D0618618

CAPTIVE COUNTESS

When Zara Silk flies into Venice to play the lead role in the film *Captive Countess*, she is instantly beset with problems. Rick Crane, the director, is openly hostile. Worse still are the threats from Wallis Bond, a fading superstar, who has her sights on playing the Countess herself. Her savage plot, to force Zara to quit, pitches the young star into a nightmare of conflict. Then, amazingly, Rick steps in to beat Wallis at her own game . . .

ANGELA DRAKE

CAPTIVE
COUNTESS

Complete and Unabridged

LINFORD
Leicester

First published in Great Britain in 2011

First Linford Edition
published 2012

British Library CIP Data

Drake, Angela.
    Captive countess. - -
    (Linford romance library)
    1. Love stories.
    2. Large type books.
    I. Title II. Series
    823.9'2–dc23

    ISBN 978–1–4448–1107–0

Published by
F. A. Thorpe (Publishing)
Anstey, Leicestershire

Set by Words & Graphics Ltd.
Anstey, Leicestershire
Printed and bound in Great Britain by
T. J. International Ltd., Padstow, Cornwall

This book is printed on acid-free paper

1

The sun was setting in a bronze glow as an ancient and splendid gondola, flanked by an escort of little rowing boats, made its way through the glittering snake of Venice's Grand Canal.

The young woman in the gondola was dressed in sixteenth-century costume; a tight-bodiced, full-skirted gown of gold and green brocade with a white ruff around her neck and fat pearls cascading across the bodice. Her waist-length black hair streamed out in the breeze. With her creamy pale skin and violet eyes she could have stepped out of a painting by Tintoretto. She seemed to embody the spirit of old Venice, whose sea-walled palaces are filled with history and the sighs of all those who have lived and loved there.

From the windows of one of the

palaces two men looked down at the gondola, noting the cries of 'Brava!' from onlookers as the young woman smiled and waved.

The taller man gave a groan of irritation. 'What a circus,' he said wearily. 'It's even worse than I'd feared.'

'Good publicity though,' his companion countered mildly.

'It's a garish, tasteless charade,' the tall man growled. 'Look at her, all decked out like some simpering Tudor wench. Why couldn't she just arrive at the airport and take a motoscafo to her hotel like ordinary people do?'

'Because she's not ordinary,' his tubby, balding companion pointed out. 'She's hot merchandise, an up and coming star, public property.'

The tall man snorted. 'I could do without all that nonsense. I just want to make a decent film.'

'Sure, you do, Rick. But you can't do that without Harry Salt's money.'

'Okay, don't rub it in. I can't do

without Salt's cash and he won't hear of any other leading lady except that trinketted-out puppet.' Rick's piercing hazel eyes glared down at the passing cavalcade.

'Have a heart, Rick. She's just a kid.'

'She's twenty-two, some women are supporting families and looking after kids at that age.' The tone of the words was dark and bitter.

'She could be a damn fine actress, though. Just because she's got a sharp publicity manager doesn't mean she's without talent.'

'Yeah, fine, I'll just have to bite the bullet and put up with all the razzmatazz. But if she thinks starring in this film is going to be about boat rides and publicity stunts she's in for a hell of a shock. Everyone on my set has to work for their money. And she's getting more than enough.'

'Just give her a chance,' the bald man said, mildly.

'Huh!' Rick pulled the window shut with a decisive thump.

'You've got to admit, though,' his friend said wistfully, still looking out of the window. 'She's one sexy lady!'

There was a pause. 'Each to his own taste,' Rick commented with more than a touch of acid.

* * *

The young woman in the gondola kept on smiling and waving, longing for the moment when she could shut the door behind her at the hotel and have some moments of quiet and solitude. She was coming to feel that there was never a moment when people were not watching her, as though even her most private thoughts were becoming public property.

But recalling that Adam, her publicity manager, had stressed the importance of gaining as much exposure to the public gaze as possible, she held her head high and smiled until her jaw ached. She wished he was here to support her, but he had been unexpectedly delayed in

London and she missed his presence keenly.

On reaching the hotel the paparazzi crowded around the entrance hall, cameras poised. 'Smile, Zara, pleeza!' they called out. 'Look this way!'

The hotel manager gave a knowing grin as he helped her out of the gondola and prepared to usher her to her suite. Zara found that the steel hoops of the wheel farthingale she wore under her skirt made it almost impossible to walk without bumping into things, but she kept smiling at the welcoming and curious hotel staff.

Alone at last in the bedroom of her magnificent suite, she tore off the punishingly heavy and constraining clothes and gave a sigh of relief, stretching like a cat. Underneath the Elizabethan costume she wore a very modern lacy bra and matching briefs. She ran her hands over the curves of her firm young body with a glow of well-being. For years she had been a plain, plump girl, to the utter despair of the brisk, kindly aunt who had shared in her upbringing.

'Such a funny little nose and such wiry unmanageable hair, whatever shall we do with you, Zara?' Aunty Kath would joke, wondering how her beautiful dead sister could have produced such a gawky child.

Zara had worried that her plainness was somehow a betrayal of the lovely, grey-eyed mother who had haemorrhaged disastrously whilst giving birth to Zara and died before her child was a day old.

It was not until Zara was sixteen that the gifts of physical beauty passed on from her mother had emerged. And yet, even now, she still did not truly believe that she was beautiful and the admiration she now attracted wherever she went sometimes made her feel like an impostor.

There was a knock on the door. Throwing on a robe, she swung the door open to find a smiling maid with her arms filled with flowers.

There was a bouquet of white roses from Adam with a card wishing her all the best for the start of filming the next day. 'Don't let Richard Crane scare you,' he had written. 'You're as good as any leading lady he's ever had the good luck to work with.'

She stroked one of the roses, reflecting on the daunting prospect of working with a top-flight director like Crane and wondering how he would rate her, a total newcomer to big-time movies.

The other bouquet was of stargazer lilies, a hugely fragrant bunch of glowing pink blooms. They were from Harry Salt, her Hollywood promoter. The message was short and sweet. 'Zara, I know you'll be perfect in your first big role, love H.'

She gave a little sigh. That the great Harry Salt should have such faith in her was rather frightening: no way could she let him down by being anything but perfect. There was such a lot at stake with this film, not just her own career but that of the director, Rick Crane. She knew that the gifted director, famed for his interpretations of Shakespeare, was risking his reputation in taking on the direction of *Captive Countess* — a huge best-seller by a popular author. If the film flopped, Harry Salt would lose millions and Crane's likelihood of being offered other projects could be severely damaged.

She hoped Rick Crane would like working with her. She had heard he was an excellent director, although stern and exacting.

She flipped her mobile open and put a call through to England.

'Zara! Hello!' Her father's voice sounded reassuringly strong and upbeat.

'Dad! How are you? Are you okay?' was her first question.

'Stop worrying, I'm doing fine. I took two whole steps today.'

'That's wonderful!'

After a disastrous fall from a horse six months ago, it had seemed debatable whether her father would ever stand unaided again, let alone walk.

'Don't get it into your head that I'm a hero! I had a physiotherapist to lean on as well as a stick, so I'm not quite ready for the London marathon yet.'

'I wish I could have been there with you,' she sighed.

'So do I,' he agreed. 'But you've got your film star career to think of now. You can't be holding your dad's hand all the time.'

'No.' She bit on her lip.

'Is that manager of yours looking after you?' he enquired.

'Oh, Adam's fine,' she reassured her father, not wanting him to guess that Adam had not yet arrived in Venice and she was very much on her own.

'Look, I don't think we should talk too long,' her father said. 'This call must be costing you a fortune.'

'No worries,' she said, thanking her lucky stars that money concerns had vanished with the dawn of her new career. After her father's accident he had had to give up his job as a senior instructor at a renowned riding centre. His pay-off had soon been used up and the two of them had been living on his state benefits and Zara's meagre salary in a repertory company. When Zara gained a regular role in an afternoon TV soap, their finances had improved a little, but when Harry Salt had noticed her, given her a screen test and signed her up, things had changed drastically. The fee Adam had negotiated for her had seemed like a lottery win.

'When do you start filming?' her father asked.

'Tomorrow morning. First thing.'

'Sounds like all work and no play.'

'Well, there is a party tonight at the hotel. The whole cast and crew will be there. And the director . . . ' She swallowed hard.

'Your first big appearance,' her father said softly. 'Are you nervous?'

She gripped the phone more tightly. 'I'll be fine,' she said. 'I've got a few butterflies, but they'll soon go.'

'The anticipation's always the worst,'

her father said comfortingly. 'Good-night, sweetheart — and good luck.'

I'll need it, Zara thought, snapping her phone shut.

She ran a bath, poured in a generous amount of Miss Dior essence, lay down in the scented water and tried to relax, wondering what it would be best to wear for the party. In the end she decided on a cream taffeta frock with puffed sleeves, a nipped-in waist and a short ruffled skirt. Adam had advised her that she should make the most of her assets of a slim figure and full breasts, but privately she considered some of the low-cut dresses and tight jeans in her new wardrobe somewhat tacky.

'There's no mileage in looking sober and discreet,' Adam had advised. 'Your film public want to see a glamorous fairytale figure, someone who seems removed from the dreary routine of everyday life.'

She slipped on five-inch heels, ran her fingers through her hair which she wore loose, then walked slowly from her suite and into the lift. Stepping out at the ground floor, she heard the buzz of conversation coming from the big salon beyond the marble reception area.

Suddenly she was conscious of feeling terribly alone, being used to having Adam hovering discreetly in the background at these glittering show-business functions. As she stood in the entrance to the salon the buzz of talk and laughter slowly stilled. Heads turned, eyes swivelled, fastening on her with interest. Her heart beat fast — then suddenly there was a burst of applause. They liked her! She felt a sudden surge of relief.

But then her glance was drawn to a solitary dissenting figure standing apart from the crowd holding a glass of red wine, running his finger thoughtfully around the rim. There was no smile on his face as he stared at her intently. In fact his expression was bleak to the point of hostility. A bitter tide of disapproval seemed to flow from him

— directly to her.

A chill ran through her. She knew this was Rick Crane, the man who was to direct her in her first big film. They should have met a few weeks before in London, but she had been forced to cancel the meeting at the last minute due to an agonising toothache which needed instant treatment. A full explanation and apologies had been sent to Crane so surely he would not hold that against her.

She tried not to think about him as she found herself drawn into an ebbing and flowing surge of people who wanted to speak to her. Curious eyes appraised her, sizing up her face and figure. The men were unanimously admiring, the women more cautious, sensing a rival. She noticed that the gathering looked glittering and wealthy, both sexes dressed in the current designer ranges, the women wearing exquisite, flashing jewellery. She recognised a number of famous faces from the world of cinema and TV. It was strange to see them in the flesh, and almost unreal to know that she was now one of them.

A waiter brought her champagne which she sipped with enjoyment. The guests talked to her with interest and kindness and gradually her confidence began to increase. Then, from the corner of her eye she was aware of Rick Crane's brooding presence. She noticed that one or two flirtatious women attempted to chat with him but received a chilly response for their efforts.

Zara became uncomfortably aware that he was only interested in observing her — and it did not look like an interest motivated by warmth or generous feelings. She felt faintly alarmed by his obvious disdain — and then decidedly annoyed. What had she ever done to make him look at her like that? She turned her back on him and determined to stop tormenting herself with speculation.

Moments later, she noticed that the group she was talking with were looking in his direction. He was coming towards her and as he did so her companions began to murmur apologies and move away.

All except one, a man of around thirty-five with thinning ginger hair and a crinkly, knowing smile. 'You two haven't met, have you?' he queried cheerily, nodding towards the approaching Rick Crane. 'Don't be put off. He comes over a touch fierce, but his bark's worse than his bite.'

Zara made herself smile. 'People keep telling me not to be frightened of him. It's making me a tad jumpy.'

The man grinned. 'You'll be okay, sweetie. I bet you'll have him eating out of your hand in no time.'

Looking up at Rick Crane now that he stood next to her, Zara was not so sure. He didn't look like a man easily swayed by feminine charms.

'Allow me to make introductions,' the ginger-haired man said to Crane. 'Zara and I have only just met, but we're already great pals.' He turned to Zara.

'This is Rick — and he and I have been mates and giving each other flak for around a million years. Rick, this is Zara who's going to make sure this damn film of yours is a great big smash hit.' His eyes twinkled. 'Oh, and I'm Benny Proctor, by the way,' he told Zara. 'Director of photography, and at your service.'

Rick Crane extended a hand to Zara, his stern hazel eyes never leaving her face. She felt her hand gripped with a steady, grim ferocity that almost made her gasp aloud.

'I was beginning to think we were never going to meet,' he observed coolly, releasing her hand which now tingled with the crushing he'd given it.

Zara was pretty sure he had been sounding her out, testing her strength to see what kind of stuff she was made of and she felt a spear of defensive antagonism. She acknowledged that he was an esteemed director and she was pretty impressed with his confident bearing and his darkly hawkish good looks. Moreover his deep resonant voice reminded her of all those National Theatre players she so admired. Even so, she had no intention of being bullied and intimidated, no matter how talented and arresting he was.

She pushed her shoulders back. 'I'm sorry I couldn't make it to our meeting in London. There was a good reason . . .'

'It doesn't matter at all, Miss Silk,' he broke in. 'I'm sure we shall understand each other perfectly once we start working together. As long as you're willing to give me one hundred percent commitment and turn in a star performance.' He gave a glinting smile, but she didn't think he was joking. A shiver went down her spine. She was new to the world of big-time acting, and although she had faith in her ability she found it hard to be challenged with such cold disdain.

She looked steadily up at him and schooled her voice to be steady and calm. 'I want to do well in this part and I'm not in the least afraid of hard work,' she told him firmly.

He raised his eyebrows. 'I'm very glad to hear it. Portraying a Venetian noblewoman will involve rather more than lying back in the glittering halo of the publicity Adam Leslie is fond of engineering for you.'

'Being the focus of a publicity exercise isn't a soft option!' she flashed back at him angrily.

He stared down at her and his face was hard and closed, sending a fresh ripple down Zara's now stiffened backbone. 'I wouldn't have thought a young woman so well endowed with such . . . natural assets as yourself would have had any opportunities to learn the differences between the hard and soft options in life,' he ventured in his deep, chocolate tones.

'Hey, steady no, Rick!' Benny murmured.

Zara threw back her shoulders once more. 'Well in that case you're very much mistaken,' she countered. 'You know nothing of my life, and you've no right to judge me. I haven't led a charmed life of ease and luxury if that's what you're thinking.'

'Fair enough, but you seem to be doing very nicely at present. And I hope your time-keeping tonight is not an indication of habitual unpunctuality. My cast and crew are expected to arrive on time, even the so-called stars.' He spat the last word out, making no attempt to disguise his contempt.

Zara took a deep breath, her eyes shining bright with the heat of her indignity. 'You won't have any reason to complain on that score, Mr Crane, once we start work.'

'Let's hope not,' he said drily.

Zara heard the scepticism in his voice. 'Just because I have a good publicity manager does not mean that I'm some kind of airheaded sex-symbol,' she pointed out.

'Your description, not mine,' he interposed with a wry smile. He had very white teeth and a wide, sensitive mouth; his smile should have been exceptionally attractive, had it not conveyed such infuriating superiority.

Zara's breathing accelerated. 'The publicity Adam arranges for me has nothing to do with my abilities as an actress,' she said.

'As we'll be getting straight into the action tomorrow I'll soon know the worst, won't I?' he replied caustically.

Zara was temporarily speechless, shocked by Crane's authoritative presumption. What an incredibly rude man! She hoped she would be able to keep her temper whilst working with him for the next few months.

Benny coughed. 'I wonder if you two undoubtedly talented folks might cease hostilities for a few moments. I'm feeling a bit battle-scarred here in the volley line.' He touched Zara's arm sympathetically. 'Take no notice, babe. Rick's always like a bear with a sore head the day before shooting starts.' He raised his glass. 'Here's to your debut, Zara. My bet is that you'll be simply terrific.'

To Zara's surprise Rick Crane also raised his glass courteously and joined in the toast, although his eyes continued to be devoid of warmth.

'Is your name really Silk?' he asked, with a touch of amused contempt.

'Yes. Did you think I invented it?' she demanded.

'No, I thought it might be the brainchild of your PR man.'

'It's my family name and I'm proud of it,' she snapped. 'And if you think you're going to scare me with your lordly disapproval and sarcasm, you're in for a disappointment.'

'I stand corrected,' he said, not sounding in the least repentant. He put down his glass. 'I think we've said all we needed to this evening. Don't stay up too late, will you, Zara. I want you costumed, made-up and on the set in the Palazzo Ceccini tomorrow at seven-fifteen promptly. Good night.' He turned on his heel and was gone.

Zara's hand trembled as she finished

the dregs of champagne.

'He really does take his work very seriously,' Benny said kindly.

'Hmm,' said Zara. 'I just hope I live to tell the tale!'

'That's the stuff,' Benny grinned. 'Don't take it to heart too much, see the funny side.'

Zara slanted a look at him. 'You didn't find it funny though, did you?'

Benny considered. 'Well, no actually I couldn't think what had got into him. He's a tough character, and he won't stand any messing about — but I've never seen him like that.'

'I don't know whether to be flattered or to pack my bags and leave right now,' Zara said with a small grimace.

'He's great to work with,' Benny said. 'You'll see another side of him altogether when we get going.'

'Let's hope so,' she agreed.

But in bed later on, her mind kept running over the meeting with Crane. Being confronted with a director who was about as friendly as a hungry barracuda was something she could have done without. She got out of bed, cranked the shutters open and leaned out of the big window. A cool, soothing breeze came from across the lagoon, softly ruffling the diaphanous white curtains.

She tried to persuade herself that Rick Crane was simply suffering from pre-shoot nerves as Benny had suggested, but somehow she felt that for some reason he truly disliked her and that he would have no compunction about making life difficult for her during filming.

Was it just because he saw her as a spoiled celebrity star with an empty head? She was too tired to work it out. Benny had said she would see another side of Crane when they started work, and she certainly hoped so. After his performance this evening she was wondering if she ever wanted to see him again.

2

The Palazzo Ceccini stood proudly above the grey-green waters of the Canal Giudecca, the reflection of its crumbling sea walls creating a second wobbly palace beneath the original.

It took twelve minutes by motoscafo, Venice's motorised, waterborne taxi service, to reach the Palace from Zara's hotel. A launch had been ordered to pick her up from the hotel at six-fifteen so that she could be in costume and make-up and on set at seven-fifteen. Rick Crane had commanded her to be on the set promptly and she had no intention of being one second late.

She got up at quarter to six and dressed in jeans and a grey silk polo neck, then called room service to request a hot chocolate. As she sipped the comforting foaming drink her mobile buzzed. She slid it open. 'Yes?'

There was a silence and then a distant voice began to speak. She heard the words General Hospital and a request to confirm that she was Zara Silk. And then the line broke up and eventually went dead.

She stared at the phone, willing it to work, knowing the call concerned her father. She dialled the number of the hospital but failed to get a connection. Looking at the absence of bars along the top of her phone display she realised the battery was flat.

She picked up the landline phone by the bedside, her knuckles white as she punched in the code for the UK. She got a connection to the hospital but when she dialled through to her father's ward there was no reply, just assorted clicks and crackles. In her mind's eye she saw the modern orthopaedic hospital in Gloucestershire where her father had spent most of the previous year, then suddenly a man's voice came through, telling her that he was the Registrar looking after her father and would she please hold the line for further information. 'Yes,' she croaked feebly, 'yes of course.'

As she waited, tension mounting, one of the reception staff knocked on the door to tell her that her motoscafo was waiting for her. Still gripping the phone, she nodded an acknowledgement.

Minutes were passing, precious minutes during which she should be getting to the Palazzo Ceccini and getting her costume on. But all she could think about was her father, imagining some accident or fall which had set his recovery back, done fresh damage to his injured body — or even placed his life in danger. After what seemed like a lifetime the man's voice spoke again. 'I'm sorry Miss Silk but it isn't possible to give you any details at the moment. We're waiting for results from the lab. Could you telephone this evening please?' The line went dead.

'Oh, don't hang up!' Zara stared helplessly at the silent phone. But clearly the call had been terminated at the other end. She would just have to wait until she finished work this evening.

Work! She looked at her watch and saw with a stab of alarm that it was now nearly seven o'clock, well over the time she should have set off. She flew down to reception and out onto the hotel's private landing where a motoscafo was waiting, its engine puttering gently.

The driver grinned at her. 'Buon giorno!' He offered a hand to help her into the boat. 'You sleepa too well, eh?'

If only it had been that simple! 'As quickly as you can, please,' she said. 'I'm seriously late.'

Delighted to oblige, the driver set off at full throttle and they sped up the canal whose waters were slowly changing from inky blue to olive green as a misty light came into the sky.

The waterside entrance to the Palazzo Ceccini was no more than a tiny landing area leading to a small door let into the ancient, disintegrating sea wall of the building. Zara raced up them, her heart pounding with apprehension. She felt that Rick Crane might materialise at any moment, his face demonic with fury at her lateness.

The whole of the palazzo had been placed at the disposal of the director and film crew for the month of October by its owner, Countess Ceccini, a great friend of Harry Salt's. Having once been in the film business herself she was sensitive to the needs of actors and had supervised the conversion of the lower section of the palazzo into dressing rooms and a small wine bar created from the entrance to the palazzo's magnificent wine vaults.

Zara found her dressing room and began stripping her clothes off with frantic haste. Her costume was laid out for her — the costume of a young aristocratic woman of Tudor times. The gown was fashioned from heavy bronze-coloured brocade. The tight bodice was long, pointed and padded at the front, high and laced at the back. Beneath the trailing skirt went several cotton petti-coats and a bulky steel farthingale. It was similar to the gown she had worn the day before when she made her spectacular entrance to Venice and she knew it took several minutes to get it all on, and that she would need help with the lacing.

As she stood in her brief lacy bra and pants she heard footsteps approaching down the stone corridor. The door was flung open and Rick Crane strode in, his eyes glinting dangerously. Waves of icy disdain flowed from him, sending a bolt of fear through Zara.

'You are hellishly late,' he informed her. 'I've got a whole cast and crew on set waiting for you. And you're not even dressed!'

Zara felt her voice choke and die in her throat. She looked down at herself, her cheeks flaming at her skimpy attire.

'Don't worry,' he said, his eyes sliding over her. 'I've seen plenty of tempting actresses' bodies. I'm not one bit interested.'

'I'm truly sorry I'm late,' she told him, desperate to make amends. 'I . . . I couldn't help it.'

'Is that so?' he said, unimpressed. His gaze held hers and his lips twitched with what looked like amused contempt.

'You're pleased, aren't you?' She drew in a sharp breath. 'You're glad that I'm late because — '

'Don't be ridiculous,' he interrupted coldly.

She was trembling with indignation. 'You're pleased because you've been proved right. You're determined to dislike me because I'm being promoted by Harry Salt. You think I'm just a silly little sex-object with no talent or commitment.'

'I couldn't have put it better myself,' he said dryly.

'How dare you?' she blazed. 'How dare you jump to conclusions when you know nothing about me? You haven't even given me a chance.'

His eyes seemed to be ripping her

into shreds. 'So what are you doing now to make me change my mind? Showing commitment? Demonstrating consideration for the crew and cast out there? All you seem to be doing is thinking of your own precious skin and how to cherish your star-quality ego!'

Zara gasped in dismay.

'Let's get things straight,' he went on, firm but calmer now. 'I'm not intimidated by temperamental stars however much box-office cash they're worth. I don't give them preferential treatment and I'm not renowned for my patience either. However I don't operate on prejudice — you'll get your chance even though you haven't made a good start. Now get dressed please, as fast as possible.'

Zara heard the sincerity in his voice beneath the sharpness. She suddenly saw how things would look to him. She was late, she was wasting time and she was behaving like a petulant child having a temper tantrum.

'I had a phone call from England

earlier,' she said softly. 'It was from the hospital where my father is at the moment. It sounded important. There were delays on the line and I forgot about the time . . . ' She looked up at him with genuine beseeching. 'I'm so sorry, Mr Crane, truly I am.'

The hardness in his eyes slowly evaporated. 'Is he going to be all right?' he enquired gently.

Zara felt a fresh lurch of panic. 'I don't know. He seemed to be doing so well. They made a special call this morning, then put me on hold. And in the end they didn't tell me anything.' She felt tears well up.

'Zara,' he said in a low voice, 'I have every sympathy with how you must feel, but there's nothing you can do about it right now, is there? So whilst this might sound harsh, you just have to put your worries out of your mind and get on with this film. Agreed?'

'Agreed.'

'Fair enough. I need you on the set now, but if you're wanted urgently to speak on the phone or even to go back to England, you'll have my full understanding and support, okay?'

She was so grateful she could have hugged him.

He gave a wry smile. 'And now, you're needed on set, Zara, so come on!'

She grabbed the cotton petticoats and began to wriggle into them with frantic haste. And then she remembered that the farthingale went on first. Flushing with agitation she started all over again.

Rick Crane went to the door and roared out down the corridor in his deep voice. 'We need a dresser here. Fast. Where the hell is everybody?' He came back into the room, cursing under his breath. 'Seems like we have total chaos on the set this morning. You'll just have to put up with my ham-handed assistance until the wretched dresser turns up.' He surveyed Zara's half-clad form. 'Right, what goes on next?'

'The bodice,' she told him, recalling that the garment had to be worn directly onto the skin and that modern underwear would show beneath the wide, low-cut neckline. Biting on her lip she reached around and unclipped her bra. The garment slipped off leaving her vulnerable and exposed.

Rick came softly behind her holding the bodice like a screen to wrap around her. 'Just stand still,' he said quietly. 'I won't take a second.'

The gentle touch of his hands surprised her, so different was it from the previous harshness of his words. And there was nothing familiar or seductive in the way his fingers brushed her skin; he was as professional as a doctor.

'Now breathe in while I tighten these laces,' he said, jerking the drawstrings firmly and making her gasp. 'Sixteenth century noblewomen were not permitted to consider their comfort,' he remarked, working his way up the bodice. 'Their waists had to appear narrow and elongated, and their breasts were flattened underneath, so as to swell at the top over the neck of the gown.' He completed his task, yanking the laces together at the top and tying the ends.

She blew out a breath, wondering how she would manage to exist for more than an hour or two in this unyielding cage.

He turned her to face him, his eyes cool and assessing. 'Can you breathe properly?' he asked briskly. 'If you can't expand your lungs fully you won't be able to use your voice with enough power on set.'

'I think so.' Thinking of the task ahead, she was suddenly overwhelmed.

He placed his hands firmly around her rib cage. 'Now breathe in, as much breath as you can manage.' She felt her ribs push against the stiff fabric as she filled her lungs with air. He frowned thoughtfully. 'Say something out loud — anything you like.'

Wow, that was some request, she

thought. She cast around and came up with some favourite lines from Keats. 'Heard melodies are sweet, but those unheard are sweeter; therefore ye soft pipes, play on . . . '

Rick lifted his eyebrows, and then he smiled. 'Well, well — not bad!'

'I think my voice is all right, don't you?' she asked anxiously.

'The voice is just great,' he said and she saw a kindle of warmth in his eyes. 'And if you can act as breathtakingly as you look, we're going to have one rip-roaring success on our hands.'

'You think so?' Her face lit up with the pleasure of being genuinely praised and valued.

'I'm sure, so don't let me down.' There was humour playing on his lips to soften the threat. A tiny electric thrill shot down her spine. She supposed it must be pre-filming nerves.

'Right,' he announced briskly. 'I want you on that set in two minutes flat. The girls can do your hair and make-up while you and the crew listen to my opening remarks, okay?' He turned at the door. 'And you can dispense with the Mr Crane bit. Call me Rick.' He looked almost friendly.

'I thought after last night that perhaps I should even call you sir.' Her eyes twinkled.

He sighed. 'I think I owe you an apology for last night. There are some things to explain. But not now, we need to get on — we'll talk later.'

She stood in front of the mirror after he had closed the door. The image looking back was so strange and unfamiliar that she felt herself beginning to lose touch with Zara Silk and be carried back in time to the Venice of the fifteen hundreds. The determination to be a success in the film lit up inside her, together with a resolve to prove herself to Rick Crane, whom she knew now was nothing like the stiff-necked bully she had at first thought.

Lifting the stiff skirts of her gown high over her calves so as not to brush them against the rough stone steps leading up to the ground floor of the palazzo, she found that the assembly were all waiting for her, their eyes curious as she went to sit in a far corner of the room where the make-up and hairdressing team were waiting for her. Soon her face was covered in a thick white foundation which was then worked gently into her skin. Her thick black hair was pinned back and hidden beneath a striking Titian-blonde wig.

As the make-up team worked, she noted Rick standing in front of the salon's stone framed window and Benny in his place with the camera crew, his face cheery and relaxed.

When Rick began to speak, complete silence fell allowing his low, resonant voice to fill the room. He made some brief comments about considering himself responsible for the well-being of everyone on the set, that he was the boss and that any problems should be addressed to him.

'Ladies and gentlemen,' he said, 'we are all here with one aim — to make a film capturing the amazing story of the *Captive Countess*. We want to recreate the atmosphere of old Venice to tell the moving story of the Countess Julietta Del Banco, an innocent girl of just fourteen who was given in marriage to her scheming, middle-aged cousin and then locked up in this very palazzo while he made plans to exchange her for the young Princess Elizabeth of England.'

Zara listened entranced as he expanded on the story of the wretched, mis-used Countess. She knew the story well, having read the best-selling novel several times. But it was not until she heard Rick Crane's interpretation that the tale became fully alive. Listening to his mellow voice describe the feelings of the frightened and bewildered Countess, she felt herself taking on the young woman's confusion and isolation.

'The story does have some threads of authenticity,' Rick told his audience. 'There was a young bride held captive in this palace in 1547, and there were manv supposed plots surrounding Elizabeth's eventual succession to the English throne. But we are not trying to produce some kind of animated text book; we are here to conjure up the feelings of an innocent but spirited young girl who finds herself terrifyingly alone in a world of greed and treachery.

'I want our audience to feel the spirit of old Venice so strongly that they can see the fog rising from the Grand Canal on a winter morning, smell the mingle of garbage and baking bread that steals through the network of the tiny backstreet canals, and feel a shiver of horror as the heroine meets her sad fate. The story revolves entirely around the heroine,' he concluded. 'Zara has a good deal of hard work ahead of her. She will need a great deal of skill and sensitivity to create a portrait of the unhappy girl-Countess . . . ' He stopped and shot Zara a penetrating look. 'I'm sure she will do it beautifully,' he finished softly.

His eyes held hers for a few moments and she felt herself filled with inspiration and spellbound by his gaze. It seemed as though he were her closest ally and all his wealth of experience and perception would be put at her disposal, so long as she was prepared to work her very hardest for him. At this moment she felt she would do anything at all that he asked her.

By now her costume and make-up were complete: a pearl-decked head-dress, hair moulded into two horn-like forelocks around her temples, face chalky-white. The make-up girl brought a hand mirror. With Rick's words ringing in her ears Zara looked at her reflection and felt a sensation of warmth tingling through every vein in her body as though she was filling up with the blood of the fourteen-year-old Countess. It was as if she had access to the girl's dreams and memories, as if she could feel the terrors of that long dead girl. For the moment she was that girl.

She got up and moved slowly to the place marked out for her under the floodlights and sat on the delicate silk-covered chair by the window overlooking the shining waters of the canal. A hush fell.

Rick looked up from his last minute perusal of the script. He had intended to give Zara some initial direction on this first scene, but he saw immediately that her concentration was intensely focused on the task ahead and that interrupting it was the last thing he should do. Silently he gestured to the film crew to finalise their angles and start the film rolling.

Zara, now living and breathing as Julietta de Banco, was keenly aware of Rick's presence, of his sharing with her the secrets of those people from the past. He was there for her both in the present and long ago. She found herself sensitive to each slight movement he made, and trusted him implicitly to guide her through her first big screen portrayal.

She knew the lines well and had practised them over and over. Now, under Rick's direction, they came alive with true meaning and feeling. She went through the entire scene without faltering, and at the end was startled back to reality by the spontaneous crackle of applause that broke out as Rick called, 'Cut!'

She blinked in the confused way one does when wakening in a strange room. Her eyes flew in search of Rick's face, needing to know if the mood she had captured so magically for herself had been felt by him too. Suddenly his approval mattered more than anything in the world and it was a crushing disappointment to find that he had been swallowed up in a small group of people wanting his advice on technical issues which had cropped up during the recording of the scene.

Feeling curiously rejected, she made her way to the coffee bar to get a drink and a bite to eat. Some of the staff and crew were already there,

43

laughing and fooling around.

'Awesome stuff, Zara,' a young guy with spiky hair called out.

'Fantastic,' said one of the make-up girls.

Presently Benny appeared and joined her at the table with his tray of coffee and doughnuts. 'Well,' he said to Zara, grinning. 'I thought you'd be good — but not that good!'

'Thanks.' She stirred her coffee reflectively. 'I hope Rick's pleased.'

'Sure. He'll be as knocked out as the rest of us. You've got to hand it to Rick. He knows how to wind actors up to make them really hum.'

'You make me sound like a mechanical toy,' she protested, laughing. As she chatted to Benny she saw a tall shadow fall over the doorway and her heart thumped in her chest. Disappointingly it was not Rick who came in, but Adam, her manager. He spotted her instantly and swooped across to kiss her. 'Zara! I'm so sorry to have been so long getting here. You know how things are, one gets tied up . . . '

'Yes, I know, it's okay,' she told him.

'You're looking simply fab-you-luss,' he commented. 'And I've already heard the opening film shots have been nothing short of spectacular.'

'Thank you,' she said.

'And speaking of shots, have a look at these,' he went on, flipping open his document case and spreading out a sheaf of photographs, showing Zara's dramatic arrival into Venice, sailing up the Grand Canal.

She had to admit the photographs did make for gripping viewing. Adam, an ex-public school boy, who always dressed in very correct dark suits and expensive shirts, had an unerring flair for the dramatic when it came to promoting his clients. When he had spotted Zara in repertory he had instantly recognized her potential for being marketed. He had seen in her a combination of innocent wistfulness and fiery sensuality that he knew could be capitalized on to the benefit of them both. He had also considered her to be a tolerably good actress. And now it looked as though his instincts were paying off, and she could see that he was in a pretty good spirits.

Benny leaned over the table, assessing the photographs with a professional and critical eye. 'There are some really good shots here,' he decided. 'But then it's difficult to get a bad angle on Zara. She's a natural.'

As the two men pored over the photographs, exclaiming in praise, Zara saw Rick walk through the door, clearly seeking her out. Instantly comprehending what was going on, he gave a knowing smile and a shrug and turned away.

Zara cursed inwardly, knowing exactly what he was thinking and how he hated the fawning publicity surrounding stardom. Besides which, she so wanted to talk to him about her performance. She endured a few moments of conflict and agitation as she tried to share in Benny and Adam's enthusiasm over a bunch of contrived snapshots, and suddenly realised that talking to Rick was far more important.

Murmuring apologies, she stood up abruptly, gathered her voluminous skirts up over her arms and hurried out of the room in search of the director.

3

When she got out into the passage Rick was just disappearing from view. She broke into a run to catch him up, woefully handicapped by her high clogs — the thick platform zocolli designed to avoid the high waters of the Venetian winters. He turned, hearing the clatter on the stone flooring.

'Steady,' he warned, as she raced up. 'I don't want you falling and breaking an ankle.'

'No,' she agreed wryly. 'That would be most inconvenient, more time and money wasted.'

'Precisely.' He lifted an eyebrow, looking at her flushed cheeks. 'You look as if you're in hot pursuit of something.'

'Yes,' she said. 'You.'

'Should I be flattered?' he smiled.

She sighed. 'Don't make fun of me. This is serious.'

'I rather got the impression that your preoccupation with your manager and his photographs was serious.

'That's unfair,' she said. 'And I don't think I deserve any more sarcasm.'

'No, probably not.' His laugh was dry and rueful.

'I simply wanted to know if you thought the first scene had gone well.'

'Very well.'

The words seemed terse and clinical. 'Did you think I was . . . okay . . . ?' she pushed hesitantly.

'Everyone was highly impressed.' His eyes had become hard again. 'Do you want me to drool and fawn, too?'

She saw that he was on edge again, presumably because of Adam's arrival with the publicity photographs. Damn! 'I just wanted to know if you were satisfied with my work. That's a perfectly reasonable thing to ask. I thought it was a director's job, to give an opinion, and I happen to value yours very highly. Is that a crime?' Her eyes flashed with feeling.

His features softened. 'No, it isn't —
and you were excellent, Zara.'

'Were you surprised?'

'Very.'

'That's hardly flattering!'

'I'm no flatterer. But I'll give praise
where it's due and you deserve it. Will
that make you happy?' She looked up at
him, sensing that he was still mocking
her. And then his face suddenly lit with
an almost playful smile. 'I was on my
way to do some research and I need to
get a move on before filming starts
again. Do you want to come?'

'Absolutely!' She felt herself caught
up in his new mood of energy.

He guided her along the passage to a
small wooden door under the main
stairway which he pushed open. 'This is
the entrance to the tower at the side of
the palazzo. You can't see it from the
main canal; its base stands in a narrow
tributary canal, or Calle as the Vene-
tians say. The outer stonework is
crumbling and I've been advised not to
use the tower for filming. But I've got a

feeling there's an atmosphere and drama about it that's too good to miss.'

As they began to climb the stone steps behind the door, Zara stumbled in the half light. Rick put out a hand to steady her. 'Hang on to me,' he said.

The stairway twisted and turned like a corkscrew and the stone was cold and slippery with moss. Zara shivered in her low-necked gown. Her eyes began to adjust to the dimness and gradually, as they went on upwards, rapiers of light glinted from the slit-like windows in the stonework.

Almost at the top of the tower there was a wooden panel in the wall barred with an iron bolt. Rick tugged at the rusting bar which had clearly not been used for years. 'Come on!' he said through gritted teeth. The iron grazed against the wood and finally gave way, allowing the panel to slide open and allow a chilly sea-breeze from the lagoon to waft into their faces. For a moment the October sun dazzled them, but within a few seconds they could pick out the edge of the harbour and the little boats with their white gusty sails.

Zara craned to look down. The height was awesome. Far below the green waters of the canal shifted and gleamed. 'Oh!' she gasped softly.

Rick shot a strong restraining arm around her. 'Do heights worry you?'

'Not especially. But this one's rather more worrying than most.'

'Worth catching on film, don't you think?'

'Yes, I suppose it is.' She looked up at him. 'Are you planning to use it?'

He looked thoughtful. 'The story doesn't tell us exactly what happened to Julietta Del Banco. It's pretty certain that she was disposed of because she knew too much, and she was not timid nor too frightened to speak out. So maybe she was sent into a convent, or overseas. Or perhaps she was murdered and dumped in the sea.'

'Poor girl,' said Zara with feeling.

'Or maybe,' Rick said slowly, 'she was

52

brought up here by her power-greedy husband and forced to jump. The suspicion and evidence of murder would be slight in those circumstances. In the unlikely event of the body being discovered, he could just put it about that she was distressed or mad and had committed suicide.'

Zara felt a chill slice through her body as she guessed what he was driving at. 'Are you planning to film that? Will you be wanting me to jump from here into the canal?'

'It would certainly make a very dramatic scene — those skirts billowing out like some exotic parachute, this fantastic wig streaming out in the wind.' His hand brushed lightly over the top of her head.

Zara swallowed. 'I don't think I would have the courage to do it,' she confessed, hoping he would not think her feeble.

His eyes crinkled with amusement. 'Directors are not in the habit of sacrificing their star attraction to the perils of air travel without a parachute or a safety net.'

She bit her lip. 'You're sending me up,' she protested. 'I'm just a newcomer to the filming game. I still believe things people say to me. I really thought you expected me to jump.'

He looked contrite. 'Oh Zara, I'm sorry. Truly I am.'

'No,' she said sadly, 'you're still having a great time getting at me. because you think I got this part just for my looks. You're wanting to cut me down to size and make me feel small.'

There was a silence. 'That's not true,' he said. 'I don't want to hurt you in any way, believe me.'

He put a hand on her shoulder and his eyes were full of kindness as he looked down at her. She felt suddenly completely at ease with him. 'Okay, I'll believe you,' she said.

'We'll get a stunt man, or throw a couple of sacks out — or just leave it to the audience's imagination.' He was still teasing, but it felt all right now she knew he was friendly again, that they were sharing a joke.

They went back down the winding staircase in companionable silence. As they approached the little door which would bring them back to their colleagues Zara said impulsively, 'You're a real puzzle to me, Rick. You were so hostile yesterday and today you were first furious and then friendly and then back to being prickly again, and then . . . '

He stiffened and raised his hands in surrender. 'Okay, you're right; I've been both boorish and unpredictable — behaving like some prima donna. I really hurt you last night, didn't I?' She nodded, her eyes wide. He ran his hands though his hair. 'Look, Zara, we need to understand each other better, but not here at the palazzo where it's all hassle and pressure, full of publicity folk and unheavenly hosts of paparazzi.'

She laughed nervously. 'No.'

'How about a drink tonight in some obscure little café? Can you escape the hotel without the press or your manager Adam Leslie following?'

'Sure. Adam's a good sort,' she added loyally. 'I owe him a lot.'

'Fine. I'll call for you at your hotel around eight.' His tone was almost tender as he stood aside courteously to let her through the door. And then he turned without pausing and strode off in the direction of the set.

★   ★   ★

That afternoon Zara worked and concentrated as she had never done before. She realised that she had no choice, that every actor and technician on the set gave Rick Crane their fullest attention. Listening to his encouragement and explanations she knew she was witnessing a master class in directing style. He was alternately tender, demanding, cajoling and sometimes on the edge of tyranny as he drew from each cast member the very best they could give.

By the end of the day, she found that her head was full of the sound of Rick's voice, and that the image of his dark head and chiselled features were carved into her inner eye. She went back to the hotel in her personal motoscafo as though in a dream.

A glow of pleasure flared inside as she reflected on the quality of her performance — better than anyone, especially herself, would ever have predicted. And the talented, hypnotic man who had brought all this about would be arriving at her door in just under an hour to take her into the magical city of Venice and give her the benefit of his undivided attention.

★ ★ ★

Back in the privacy of her suite Zara took a quick shower and then called the hospital in Gloucestershire and asked to speak to the doctor overseeing her father's care. Her currently buoyant mood instantly evaporated as the difficulties of the morning repeated themselves with a lengthy series of clicks and buzzes which completely dominated the connection. Eventually the cool-voiced doctor who had spoken to her earlier came on the line. 'Have you got the results from the lab?' she asked anxiously.

'Yes, we have some results now, Miss Silk.' There was a silence and she gripped the receiver in frustration. 'I rather think this is information that should not be given over the phone,' the voice said carefully.

'I'm in Venice. There's no way I can speak to you in person,' she pleaded. 'Is he all right?' A dark alarm seized her. 'He's not . . . dead is he?'

'He is alive, Miss Silk — and perfectly well so far.'

Zara was now convinced something was badly wrong. But what? Why was this man being so unhelpful? 'I'd like to speak to my father please,' she said, her voice clipped and sharp.

'He's asleep now. I would advise you

to call again in the morning. Goodbye, Miss Silk.' The line was cut.

Zara could not believe what was happening. She sat on the bed, perplexed and seriously worried. Time passed as she wondered what she should do next, and when the door buzzer sounded her body jerked with shock. Dazed, not really thinking of anything except her father's condition so many miles away, she walked abstractedly to the door and opened it.

Rick stood there, relaxed and assured looking in well cut jeans and a thick cotton sweater. 'Am I too early?' he asked gently.

'No, come in.' She walked back into the room, touching her hair which was still damp from the shower and moving around her face in an unruly black halo. She was aware of Rick observing her carefully. 'Please,' she said in a hurried distracted voice, 'sit down while I finish getting ready.'

He put out his hand and caught her arm as she turned to go to the bedroom. 'Zara, what's wrong?'

She looked up at him and sighed. 'It's my father. I still can't get in touch.'

'The signal strength can vary a lot around here,' he said.

'No. I got a connection, but the man I spoke to wouldn't tell me anything. In fact he was rather strange — not like a doctor at all.'

Rick frowned. 'Look, you're clearly pretty exhausted, and you've had a hell of a day.'

'No,' she broke in. 'I'm not imagining all this, and I'm not hysterical and overwrought if that's what you were wondering.' She closed her eyes in frustration and despair. When she opened them she saw that his face was filled with concern and tenderness. 'Oh, Rick! There's something terribly wrong.' He drew her to him and put his arms around her, holding her with calming reassurance. When she eventually pulled away, her eyes were pink and swollen. 'Sorry,' she whispered. 'I'll pull myself together.'

'Is there any way I can help?' he asked.

'I don't know, Rick. I need time to think things through.' She stared miserably ahead, feeling utterly helpless.

'Would you rather not go out?' he asked. 'Would it be better if I left?'

'No. I want you to stay — and I want to go out, too. Sitting here brooding is making me jumpy.' She gave him a small rueful smile.

'All right then, let's go out and see the glories of Venice.' He took her down into the lobby, his hand under her elbow, his face defying anyone to stop and remark on their having spotted the up-and-coming Zara Silk in her jeans and without make-up setting out in a privately hired motoscafo with her Svengali director Rick Crane.

Rick had engineered things carefully, ordering the boat to wait on the landing area of the villa next door to the hotel where no paparazzi were lurking. They sped up the Grand Canal, under the

61

Rialto bridge and then turned off into the network of small narrow waterways intersecting the two main canals. Zara looked in wonder at the old villas and warehouses bordering the water, at the massive sea-stained walls whose reflections shimmered in the trembling water under an aubergine-coloured evening sky. Pigeons cooed in ripe sing-song tones and bells sounded from dozens of churches. She shivered with the magic of it all.

'Venice,' mused Rick. 'Half eastern, half western: one foot in Europe, the other in Asia.'

'So fragile,' Zara said. 'A city drowning in the sea.' She trailed her fingers in the water.

'Oh, I think the Serenissima has a few years to go yet.'

They went to a café lit with lamps from old gondolas. Rick ordered two glasses of Barolo and guided Zara to a table overlooking the canal.

She sipped the dark, full wine gratefully and began to relax a little.

'Feeling better?' Rick asked.

'Yes.' But she knew now that she mustn't delay telling him of the decision she had been forming in her mind over the last hour. 'Rick,' she said carefully, 'If I don't get some positive news about my father tonight, and if I can't make contact, I think . . . ' Her face was stricken as she looked at him.

'You'll have to go back to England,' he concluded quietly.

'Yes. Will you be dreadfully angry?'

He turned away briefly. 'Oh hell,' he muttered. 'Yes, of course I'll be angry, but with fate, Zara, not with you.'

Tears sprang into her eyes. 'Oh, Rick, thank you!' she burst out.

Suddenly their glances were drawn to the door as a colourful group of people burst into the café with a great deal of fuss and noise. Although some of them wore exotic Venetian face masks, it was clear they were not a Venetian crowd as they were joshing together in English.

The centre of attraction was a tall blonde who seemed vaguely familiar to

Zara. She was dressed in a clinging silver cat-suit festooned with zips and tiny mirrors that shimmered as she moved. She was carrying a silver motorcycle helmet and reflective goggles. Every single head in the café turned.

Rick gave a groan. 'That's Wallis Bond; Queen of the American soaps. She certainly knows how to get noticed.'

Wallis looked around the room with the predatory glance of an animal that hunts and kills to survive. 'Zara Silk!' she exclaimed in a deep husky voice, advancing swiftly in the direction of Rick and Zara's table.

'Darling,' cried Wallis, turning her huge eyes on Zara. 'I've been dying to meet you ever since Harry told me about your role in *Captive Countess*.' Her sapphire blue eyes sparkled with a vivacity that was not wholly friendly. Wallis reached across the table, her hand extended in greeting, and in her exuberance, she somehow managed to knock Zara's glass over and the dark liquid shot into Zara's lap, making her spring up in concern.

'Are you okay, Zara?' Rick's face was tight with annoyance as he glanced across to Wallis.

'Oh, no! I'm so sorry.' Wallis assumed an expression of intense contrition. 'Sweetie, let me clean you up a bit.' She reached for a paper napkin but Zara swiftly excused herself and made for the washroom.

As she splashed water onto her wine-soaked jeans the door to the washroom opened and Wallis Bond pushed her way in, turning to close the door and then slide the bolt across, locking them both in.

Instantly Zara's instincts told her to be wary and on the alert. 'That wasn't an accident, was it?' she asked in a low voice.

'I'm afraid not darling. Just a ploy to get us two together for a cosy chat.'

'Well?' Zara enquired coldly, feeling her face instinctively harden. 'What do you want?'

'Oh, I do like a girl who gets straight to the point,' Wallis drawled in her heavy Texan accent. 'And what I want is your part in *Captive Countess*.'

Zara almost burst out laughing, the statement was so ludicrous. But noting the splinter-sharp expression in Wallis's eyes she realised she needed to take the menacing blonde very seriously. 'You might want it, Wallis,' she said coolly, 'but you're not going to get it.'

Wallis's full lips twitched. 'Oh but I am, darling Zara. I most surely am.'

Zara suddenly felt chilling fear, an overwhelming sense of evil at work.

'You're going to give it me on a plate, sweetheart,' Wallis continued.

Zara swallowed hard before retorting, 'Nothing would make me do that.'

Wallis lifted an eyebrow. 'Not even daughterly love?'

Zara involuntarily staggered against the wash basin and the cold porcelain cut into her back. 'What?'

'Love for your father in a little hospital in England. In the Cotswolds I believe. You have such cute names for your country places. I gather he's not been too great recently.'

'How do you know all this?' Zara whispered in terror.

'I have a little team of loyal supporters doing reconnaissance work for me overseas in your quaint Cotswolds,' smiled Wallis. 'I think you may have spoken to one of them earlier. I hope his English accent was convincing.'

'The Registrar! I knew he was a fake — one of your team?' Zara felt she was living in a nightmare.

'Uh-huh. Totally reliable. He's done one or two other jobs for me before.'

'You're crazy,' Zara gasped.

'No, just desperate to have that part. And rich and clever enough to know how to get it, darling.'

'You're sick . . . evil . . . '

Wallis smiled. 'This is the big time you're in now, Zara. We don't keep our knives in sheaths. But no one is going to get hurt so long as you do as you're told . . . by me, that is.'

Zara looked down at the floor in disbelief. 'So you're telling me that unless I hand over my role to you, then all kinds of unpleasant things might happen to my father?'

'Got it in one, babe.' Wallis looked down at her with mocking pity. 'It's not difficult to arrange rather convincing mishaps if you employ professionals, as I do. And I'm a pro myself, of course. I've been in this shark-infested business for a long time and my teeth have had to grow very sharp.'

Zara was no fool. She understood now what the mysterious phone conversations and erratic connections meant — and that her father would be entirely helpless if Wallis decided to play really rough. Moreover, she saw that Wallis would go to any lengths to secure this part.

An urgent knocking sounded on the door. Other customers were wanting to use the facilities.

'Decision time,' Wallis drawled in the satisfied tones of one who knows she holds all the cards.

'There's no decision to be made,' Zara said miserably. 'Tell me what I have to do.'

4

Wallis smiled. 'That's the spirit, darling. Now the first thing you are going to do is ditch the fascinating Rick Crane and come along with me to a gorgeous party where all the Beautiful People will be gathered.

'He'll be furious.' Zara shuddered at the thought.

'Exactly,' Wallis commented. 'His opinion of you will sink like a stone. Such a shame for you, darling, but rather good news for me.'

Misery lodged in Zara's chest as she trailed behind Wallis back out to the café and the table where Rick sat waiting.

'Zara's just fine and dandy now, all cleaned up!' Wallis cooed to Rick.

'Good.' Rick's face was impassive. 'Well if you'll excuse us, Miss Bond, Zara and I have some business to discuss.' He glanced at Zara, waiting for her sit down and join him again.

Wallis chuckled. 'Oh, Zara's coming along to a party with me. It's all fixed up. She couldn't resist it, could you darling?' A silver-clad arm clasped itself against Zara's waist. The pressure from Wallis's hard fingers gave instructions as firm and bold as those of a sergeant major.

Zara bit down on her lip. 'Would you like to come too, Rick?' she asked with mute appeal.

He frowned, trying to work out what was going on. 'I thought we had an engagement to get to know each other a little better,' he said pointedly.

Zara felt her heart tighten as she stood mute and helpless.

'Zara needs to be in the limelight,' Wallis fluted. 'She's far too charming to be hidden away in a little backwater like this.'

'So where are you going?' Rick enquired coldly, ignoring Wallis and staring hard at Zara.

She swallowed. 'To meet some friends of Wallis's,' she offered lamely.

'Why don't you join us, Rick?' Wallis enquired. 'Everyone will be there.'

'I don't go to parties when I'm working,' he replied shortly. 'And we have an early start in the morning.' Again he probed Zara's face with cold and questioning eyes.

Zara felt a sense of awful betrayal, as though she were deserting a trusty ally and joining the ranks of the enemy. But if the safety of her father was at stake, she really had no choice. And she had no doubt whatsoever that Wallis would play very dirty to get what she wanted.

'Fine,' Rick said, getting up and laying some money on the table. 'Enjoy yourself, Zara,' he said with a grim smile of farewell. 'I'll see you in the morning. Punctually this time, please.' He strode from the café and disappeared into the bustle of the square outside.

'The pompous bastard!' Wallis drawled. But there was a light of admiration in her eyes as she watched Rick's departure.

Zara found herself in some kind of horrible dream as Wallis steered her into a silk-curtained gondola. It was dark now and she could see other gondolas slithering through the narrow waterway, dark and shimmering in the moonlight, the water beneath them a bluish black. In other circumstances she would have been entranced by the beauty of it all.

'Cheer up, sweetie,' Wallis chided. 'You'll love it at the party.'

'You've no need to play cat and mouse with me,' Zara said stonily. 'Just tell me what I have to do to make sure my father is safe.'

'All in good time,' Wallis said, clearly enjoying herself. She trailed her long fingers in the water. 'Is Rick Crane always such a killjoy?' she asked.

'He takes his work very seriously,' Zara said.

'Mmm. So calm and cool. So very . . . English. I think I'd like to see him get a little ruffled . . . '

'He's not always calm and cool,' Zara said, feeling Rick was under attack and rushing to his defence.

'Really? You seem to know a quite lot about him. Tell me, have you slept with him yet, darling?'

Zara flushed. 'No.'

'He looks as though it might be worth trying him out.'

'I doubt if you'll get the chance,' Zara said in a voice of ice. 'He doesn't go for gloss and glamour. He likes people to be committed to their roles, work hard, be professional.'

'Know their lines, always be on time,' Wallis interrupted.

'Yes.' Zara realised she had allowed herself to give away far too much.

'So now we know how to make sure you get right up darling Rick's nose. Fluff your lines, turn up late . . . ' Wallis said, obviously delighted with her newfound knowledge.

Zara groaned internally with dismay. 'When Harry told me that Rick

Crane was going to direct *Captive Countess* I knew I wanted that part more than anything I've wanted before,' Wallis said, suddenly deadly serious and direct. 'I've seen one or two of his productions at the National. He's a genius. And I'm at a stage in my career when I'm ready to make the fullest use of that calibre of director talent.'

'And I'm not?' Zara enquired.

'You're just a kid. He's wasted on you. In any case Harry more or less promised me the part — until he saw Adam Leslie's damn portfolio of you.'

Zara was trying to piece things together. 'Have you worked with Harry Salt before?'

'I've lived with the guy for the last four years, darling. And I've always had the plum parts — until now.'

'But Mr Salt's not going to change his mind about the casting, is he? Whatever you do?' She knew she was clutching at straws, but what else was there to clutch at?

'Once you prove yourself a total

disaster — which of course you will — he'll give me the part on a plate, sweetie-pie. In fact he'll be falling over himself to get me. With you out of the way, there'll be a full-scale set idle and eating money and just crying out to be used. Harry hates waste. And I'll be right here to step in.'

'Rick won't stand for it,' Zara said stubbornly.

Wallis's eyes glittered. 'He'll do as Harry says. Think about it, darling, Rick has no real clout — he's not the one putting up the money.' She paused. 'And if you think I'm past it, you can think again. I can still swing things the way I want; both man and money-wise.'

Her heart thundering, Zara stayed silent for the rest of the journey.

The boatman stopped outside a palazzo from which music and light blazed. Wallis led the way up a marble staircase guiding Zara into a huge salon decorated entirely in pearly white paint and furnished with black leather furniture and Venetian glass lamps. The style was stark and minimal, embellished with just one large painting by Picasso over the magnificent fireplace. Zara hated the place on sight. Looking around the crowded salon she saw many faces that she knew: film stars, pop stars, fashion designers and a couple of European royals. The jet set out in force. It was like being in Madame Tussauds, only everyone was moving.

'Champagne, darling? A little something to eat?' Wallis gestured to tables lining the side of the room where the display of food was so imaginative it seemed a crime to think of eating it. There were glazed whole ducks, bread curled and braided like a Regency coiffure, marzipan gondolas and a huge cake in the shape of the palazzo.

'I'm not hungry,' Zara whispered.

'Never mind,' Wallis said, taking brimming champagne flutes from a passing waiter and handing one to Zara. 'Just drink this lovely stuff.' Glass in hand she then hauled Zara around the room introducing her to group after group of curious faces until Zara was exhausted. This seemed like the longest and most drama-filled day of her life. For a moment she wondered where Rick had gone and if he would follow her. A spark of hope quivered within but she knew she was being foolish and sentimental.

Wallis would not let her out of her sight. She was as attentive as a jealous lover and vigilant as a hawk. And seemingly tireless.

'You've made your point, Wallis,' Zara said, when hours had dragged by. 'I have to get some sleep. Any more of this and I won't even be up to acting the part you've mapped out for me.'

'Okay, sweetheart. I think we understand each other now.' She led Zara back down the stairs where a motoscafo was already waiting. 'If you call the hospital at eight I think you'll find your father available to speak to you,' she said in a matter-of-fact voice. 'Don't bother calling earlier, or you'll find there's only the rather unhelpful 'doctor' to speak with. Get it?'

'Oh, yes — I get it,' Zara said bitterly.

'After that you'll have to get to the Ceccini palazzo, get into costume and have your make-up done. I don't think you stand much chance of being on the set much before nine. Rick should be nice and mad by then.'

Oh no, thought Zara. *If only this was nothing but a bad dream and I could wake myself up.*

'And don't forget to act really dumb, darling, will you? I don't want anyone to tell me the sweet new bimbette movie star knows her lines backwards. I don't want to hear anything about her wonderful concentration and the way she hangs on Rick Crane's every word and starts to live the role of the Countess. Comprenez?'

'Yes,' said Zara, dulled and crushed with fatigue and misery.

'I'll be watching your every move, of course,' was Wallis's parting shot as the boat's engine roared into life. 'I have my spies on the set, so don't think you can go sneaking behind my back being a good little girl for Rick.'

★　★　★

Back at her hotel Zara flew through the lobby with tears stinging her eyes. She undressed and lay in bed, trembling with delayed shock. She wondered if she had capitulated too easily to the demonic Wallis Bond.

Should she call the police, in England? In Venice? Should she call Rick and tell him everything? She yearned to be honest with him and seek his support, but something told her it would be truly dangerous to make any deviation from Wallis's instructions — at least for the present. Wallis had the scent of blood in her nostrils; she was wild and desperate and Zara felt certain she was capable of anything to get what she wanted.

Eventually Zara fell into an uneasy sleep. She woke at six, longing to be up and about, making her way to the Ceccini palazzo, working once again with Rick, drawing inspiration from his compelling direction, co-operating with him in the creation of a beautiful work of art.

She went to the window, opened the shutters, and watched the white fog drifting in from the lagoon, and a pale silver sun rising. The delicious fragrance of freshly baked bread mingled with the salt breeze. How could you watch an autumn dawn in Venice and not feel your heart lift? But all this loveliness had been spoiled for her. She sat hunched and miserable as the minutes dragged by until eight o'clock. At regular intervals the reception desk staff called to remind her, oh so politely, that her motoscafo was waiting for her. Almost weeping, she would explain that she was not yet ready to come down.

Just after eight she punched in the hospital's number and was soon hearing her father's cheery voice on the line. 'Oh Dad! Thank God!' she exclaimed without being able to stop herself.

'Hey — what's the problem, love?' he chuckled.

'You sound so well,' she said.

'I am, love. I'm doing fine. Never better. What about you?'

'Oh, I'm good too. Everything's going well.' She winced at the lie, but no way must he know the truth.

'I've got this new doctor,' her father said. 'Nice chap, young and very bright. He's from the States. He's thinking up some new treatments for me.'

Her heart sank like a stone. Finally she had to accept that Wallis was really in earnest, not just playing a cruel game, and that what she had told Zara was all true.

Her father chatted a little more about his new doctor and some of the patients he had made friends with. Zara forced herself to go through the conversational motions which would prevent her father catching wind of the dreadful situation she found herself in.

When she eventually stepped into her

motoscafo she was already an hour and a half late. Her head ached from the champagne Wallis had insisted she drink and she felt dulled and drained.

All in all the prospects for the day ahead were decidedly bleak.

★　★　★

'I think you might be about to fall victim to the wrath of the gods,' Benny Proctor whispered to Zara as she approached the door of the palazzo's main bedroom where filming was to take place that morning. He was checking camera angles in the doorway. He looked as though he was just dying to get on with some action.

'I suppose I've held everything up,' Zara said lamely.

He gave her a wry look. 'You could say that.'

She longed to say that she couldn't help it, terribly hurt to realise she had dropped down a few notches in Benny's esteem. But the secret had to be kept, the act preserved. She gave a non-committal smile.

'Rick's gone to grab a coffee,' Benny said. 'I think the gall kept rising in his throat. I'll go let him know you're here.'

'Yes, all right,' she murmured.

'Is there anything else you'd like me to tell him?' Benny asked. 'Maybe even at this late hour I might be able to save you from being flayed alive.'

Zara stared at him in despair. 'No.'

Shrugging his shoulders Benny went off to find Rick.

Zara drew her silk robe around her. This morning they were shooting a brutal and sexy bed scene and she wore only a cotton nightgown under her robe and her wig was worn long and loose. She felt exposed both physically and psychologically as she moved forward into the room and felt curious and critical eyes rest on her.

She saw that her screen husband Boris Linton was sitting on the magnificent canopied bed which dominated the room. It was made of dark, heavily carved walnut, draped with burgundy silk. Boris was wearing a silk dressing gown and unconcernedly reading the morning paper whilst swinging a languid foot to and fro. He glanced up and smiled when he saw her. Zara realised that Boris must have seen it all before; temperamental stars, lateness, tantrums, shooting schedules not met. It made no difference to him at this late stage in his career. He'd already got his millions made and if *Captive Countess* turned out to be a fiasco, it was no skin off his nose.

Zara stood waiting for Rick as though awaiting a death sentence. As footsteps came down the corridor, her heart began to thump. Rick came in and walked to stand under the window, a copy of the script in his hand. Not once did he glance in Zara's direction. Not for a moment did he give any sign of anything being amiss.

Rick's apparent disinterest was more shattering than anything Zara could have imagined. And as she began to feel the pain of his rejecting indifference, she was suddenly struck with the incredible knowledge that she was already in love with him. Colour flared in her face and her hand flew up in a swift involuntary movement to press against her breast bone.

Already he was speaking about the scene they were about to enact. A complete silence fell as he began to tell them the story of the young Countess's wedding night. He explained that girls of the nobility in the sixteenth century were often married very young to much older men for reasons of social status or money. Many of these innocent, virgin girls were subjected to brutal and painful ordeals from elderly, often drunken bridegrooms. He invited the cast to consider Julietta Del Banco's plight and to feel with her the nightmare of that first night with her husband.

Zara gazed at Rick, transfixed by his eloquence. He was hypnotic, he totally eclipsed any other man she had ever met. His voice seemed to carve itself into her senses, every nerve in her body strained to respond to him.

Despite herself, despite Wallis Bond's threats, despite the safety of her dear father, Zara felt herself once again merge into the spirit of the long dead Countess Del Banco, to fill up with the spirit and essence of the dead girl. She lay on the bed with her head on the frilled pillows and she became the Countess once more, experiencing all the hell that young girl had suffered on her horrific wedding night at the mercy of the ageing and debauched Count.

Towards the end of the scene as Boris Linton clawed at the front of her nightgown tearing it straight down the front and exposing her breasts, she lost herself in her own misery, allowing all her despair to show on her face and in her tear-rimmed eyes.

Zara lay back on the pillows, suddenly cold with foreboding. She had let herself go, obeyed her instincts, done exactly the opposite of what Wallis had decreed. What awful thing might happen now?

Rick had cut the scene and looked across to Zara. 'That was a very moving performance,' he said softly with deep sincerity. 'Are you okay?'

She felt his presence acutely and could not bear to look at him. She must never give him a performance like that again. Not in this film, anyway. And after the mess she was going to have to make of the rest of it, there probably wouldn't be any chance of ever working with him again. Her life seemed to be dissolving into ruins.

Rick's eyes burned down into hers and the concern and questioning in them caused tears to spring up beneath her eyelids. 'Come with me for a coffee and a debriefing session,' he instructed. 'We need to talk.'

Zara knew he was referring more to last night than the scene she had just completed. She saw how much he was prepared to forgive. She turned her head away in despair. 'No, I don't want to.'

'Zara, come on. Don't play games.' He was so kind and cajoling she felt she would split open with torment and guilt.

'I don't want a coffee. I'll just stay here until the next scene,' she persisted, her eyes fixed on the rich pattern of the bedcover.

'Zara, look at me!' he commanded. The call of her name in that deep, compelling voice gave her no choice but to raise her head and allow his shrewd eyes to assess her. 'I could have killed you last night,' he said in a matter of fact voice. 'Falling for the lure of the glitterati, ditching me for the bright lights of Wallis's party.'

She stared at him, her eyes full of hurt.

''Everyone will be there',' he quoted with a wry smile, perfectly capturing Wallis's husky drawl with his uncanny facility for mimicry. 'And then to be so late this morning. I had to make sure I would be out of the way when you finally showed up so I wouldn't wring your lovely neck!'

He was giving her every chance to explain what had happened. He wanted to think the best of her. He wanted to believe that her actions had been prompted by more noble motives than wilful self-centredness. Which was in fact the truth, she reflected wretchedly.

But she could not tell him the truth. The stark reality of Wallis's intention to carry out her threats had become more vivid and substantial as the hours went by. Zara was entirely convinced that Wallis was truly dangerous.

She gazed at Rick and could not think of anything to say to him. With massive-self control she drove all the anguished appeal out of her eyes and forced her face to assume an expression of blank indifference.

Rick frowned. She could tell that he was asking himself what was going on. 'Did you contact your father this morning?' he asked sharply.

'Yes, he's fine.'

'No further cause for concern, then?'

'No.' She was painfully aware of the brittleness of her smile as she answered him. She hated herself.

'Well, that's good news at any rate, which is more than I can say for your apparently transformed attitude to your work, and to me.' His eyes were hard and glinting now, just as they had been on that first challenging meeting. Again he paused, giving her one more chance to offer him some enlightenment. Again she schooled herself to be silent, and felt as if she were drowning in a bath of misery.

He straightened up, his face closed and glacial. 'Okay, I'm hearing loud and clear that you want me to keep my distance. Fair enough,' he said bitterly. 'But just make sure the standard of work doesn't change, and if you dare turn up late again, I can't begin to describe what my reaction will be.'

Zara waited until he was well occupied with all the other people

91

demanding his attention, then slunk off to her dressing room and laid her head on the little dressing table in despair.

She knew there was no point trying to think things out. She had been told quite clearly by Wallis what to do, and the only thing that concerned her was how to do it. That was indeed a considerable problem, given that Rick was asking her just as clearly to do exactly the opposite.

And when she was in his hypnotic presence, she seemed to have difficulty thinking of anyone or anything else.

It had not escaped her that his words suggested the possibility of his feelings towards her reaching beyond a professional interest. The idea that he might be feeling for her what she was feeling for him was heady and seductively delicious. But in the present circumstances, it could be nothing more than an added complication in already impossible circumstances.

She was going to have to take an extremely tight grip on herself.

A gentle knocking on the door announced Adam's arrival. He drew up a chair and sat beside her, smiling as she carried out some necessary repair work on her face with an assortment of cosmetics.

Adam looked on, charmed by the magic women could create from little tubes and bottles of prettily scented substances. 'You're doing really splendidly in this film, Zara,' he congratulated her.

'Mmm.' Zara busied herself with an eyebrow pencil, sensitive to Adam's admiration and dismayed at the thought of his being yet another liked and trusted person she would be forced to deceive.

'What's the matter?' Adam asked with friendly concern. 'Rick Crane isn't still posing problems, is he? He does have a reputation as a tough director.'

'Things are fine with Rick,' she cut in firmly.

'Excellent. By the way, I heard on the grapevine that you were at a showbiz party with Wallis Bond last night.' He was beaming with approval that she was getting some excellent publicity.

'Yes,' she confirmed tight-lipped. 'It was like stepping into the pages of a celebrity magazine with everyone in motion.'

'Well, I've got a rather interesting proposition to put to you.'

She stiffened. 'Go on.'

'I've had an enquiry from Ramana, an Italian design label. 'They wondered if you would model swimwear for them while you're in Venice.'

'But I've no experience in modelling. I'm an actress,' she said.

'You're a star,' he reminded her. 'You can do anything you want. And you happen to have a beautiful figure, which a great many people would like to admire. They are offering a considerable fee, and of course the boost to your popularity will be enormous. The locations they're suggesting are very appealing — The Bridge of Sighs, the Lido . . .'

'Oh, Adam, I don't know.' Her face

was hunted and anxious. Her thoughts had instantly flown to Rick's view of this offer. Posing for half naked pictures! His regard for her would sink even lower than it was now.

Adam opened out a draft contract and laid it on the table for her inspection. It occurred to her that now she had lost all chance of Rick's esteem, it seemed almost unbearable to disappoint Adam as well.

'All right — I'll do it,' she said, lacking all enthusiasm.

'Super!' Adam exclaimed. 'Good for you.' As he began to talk through the logistics of the proposed photo shoot the door opened and Wallis Bond slipped in, as lithe and sinuous as a reptile. Today she was swathed in beige leather as soft as a baby's skin, though her heavy, clanking jewellery was more in the class of weaponry than adornment.

The hairs stood up on the back of Zara's neck.

Spotting Adam, Wallis gave a radiant

smile. 'Ciao!' she purred. 'We met at a party in London way back in the summer, remember?'

'Well, hello there, great to see you again.' Adam leapt up and kissed her on both cheeks.

'I just had to come and pay my respects to the rising star here,' Wallis said beaming at Zara. 'She's sensational — I'm positively dazzled.'

'She is indeed,' Adam agreed, playing the part of the perfect English gentleman which he knew would charm the American superstar Wallis.

'I heard you were just spell-binding this morning, darling.' Wallis said.

Zara swallowed. 'Thank you.'

'But it can be hard to keep things at that level. When you've been in the film business as long as I have, you know there are lows along with the highs.' Wallis shot her rival a rapier-like glance, as if the dangerous undertone to her voice was not enough. 'So don't be worried if you find your inspiration flagging a little this afternoon.' She turned to address Adam. 'And of course, poor Zara has all this worry about her father. I gather he could be in quite a bad way.'

Adam looked concerned. 'Has your father taken a turn for the worse?'

'Well . . . ' Zara felt as though she were choking.

'Zara told me a little about him when we bumped into each other yesterday,' Wallis broke in helpfully. 'But I hear he's in good hands — under close supervision. Isn't that right, darling?' Her gaze fastened on Zara, and the atmosphere was filled with soft menace.

'Well, that's good to know,' Adam said, seeming not to notice there was anything wrong. He got to his feet. 'I really must be on my way. Things to do, people to see . . . ' He put a gentle hand on Zara's shoulder and then was gone, leaving her alone with the snake-like superstar.

Wallis gave a low, husky laugh. 'I'm not going to fence with you, darling. You're still just a novice; it wouldn't be fair to line you up with an old hand like me who knows how to play real rough. It's a cruel world, Zara honey, and from now on you're going to do what I say.'

'Is my father all right?' Zara murmured, her heart beating with fear.

'So far. But contingency arrangements have already been made. I'm prepared to overlook this morning, but from now on your acting talents are going to be used to make sure you play the part of the dumbest rising star on the planet. I want Harry tearing his hair out and Rick ready to commit murder — and you off that set as soon as possible.'

5

Zara sat in her dressing room, chewing on her lip and imagining herself going back on to the set and working under Rick's direction in which her role was to act like a spoiled and wilful child. She knew she could not go through with it. She could not be in his presence and not be influenced by his quiet, yet total authority, his capacity for making it possible for her to crawl under the skin of another person. More important still she could not bear to show herself to him in a bad light.

Escape and flight seemed the only other avenue open. She changed out of her costume, put on her jeans and a heavy sweater against the sharp chill in the Venetian October air, and having checked there was no one in the corridor, made her way stealthily out of the palazzo. She thought it best not to make use of the boat available for the cast and crew and instead wound her way round the land side of the building, cutting into the ornate garden of a neighbouring palazzo and finding her way to its waterside from where she hailed a passing gondola.

She remembered the little café where she and Rick had started their exploration of each other's personalities before being abruptly interrupted by the intervention of Wallis Bond. The memory prompted a sudden urge to go there again, and after lightly springing from the gondola she made her way through the square to the café and sat down at the table she and Rick had occupied only the day before.

Sipping a cappuccino she became lost in contemplation of the impossible situation in which she found herself. Eventually she reached the conclusion that the only sensible thing to do was to resign from her part in the film. At least then she would not have to go through the humiliating charade of acting and behaving so badly that she would be dismissed.

Wallis's threats were only too real, and her father's safety was precious to her. There was no choice but to throw up her fantastic leading part in the film. At least she would be acting with dignity and Wallis would not have the satisfaction of seeing her ruin her professional reputation. Nor would Rick be forced to believe his original ideas of her being no more than a cleverly marketed pretty girl with negligible acting talent and little commitment.

Having come to this decision Zara rallied a little from the pit of despair into which she had been sinking since Wallis's arrival in her life. She ordered another coffee and a chocolate-filled pastry.

As she nibbled at the pastry her eyes were suddenly drawn to look up. She had the strange feeling that she was being watched, and while she was becoming used to being the object of many curious glances, this feeling was different. She felt that someone was compelling her to look up, almost hypnotising her to pay attention. She knew there was only one person who could have that effect on her, and her pulse raced as she raised her head.

He was sitting opposite her, alone, simply watching. There was a glass of brandy on the table in front of him and his long fingers were stroking it thoughtfully, while his penetrating eyes made a careful appraisal of Zara's face. He did not smile, merely raised a grim, questioning eyebrow.

Zara was aware of a blush flushing her face. She felt a spark of panic flare inside. She stood up and as if in a dream walked across to his table.

'Sit down,' he said softly. Still there was no smile on his face or in his eyes. There was no anger either, just cool resolve.

'How did you know I was here?' she said, her voice unsteady.

'I followed you. I had the feeling you

might take flight, so I kept a close watch on what you were doing.'

'That's stalking,' she protested.

'No. In my book it's simply finding out what's going on with my leading lady and protecting her — most probably from herself.' She stared at him in fascinated apprehension. She might have guessed she would not escape from him so easily. 'You're supposed to be on the set now, Zara. We're shooting the first scene between you and your illicit lover; the appealing young manservant who brought about the final downfall of the unlucky Countess. Remember?'

'Yes.' Her voice was as soft as a sigh.

'Good. I'm glad some things are still registering in that pretty head of yours. So why are you here, drinking coffee and playing truant?' She gazed at him, dumb and helpless, thinking she knew how a trapped rabbit felt. 'Haven't you learned the lines?' he enquired coolly.

'Yes . . . no . . . ' *Oh, please God, help me,* she was praying.

'Do you or don't you know the lines?'

'Yes.'

'Well for that at least I must be grateful. So something else must be wrong,' he persisted with relentless logic.

'Nothing's wrong,' she protested, wincing at the lies and deceptions she was being been forced into.

He leaned forward. 'So why are you behaving like a first class idiot?'

She made her face assume a stubborn and mule-like look as she refrained from answering.

With a swift gesture of angry frustration, he drained his glass. Then he stood up, reached over the table and pulled her to her feet. 'Come on. It's too public here. The paparazzi are already sniffing around. I can see the headlines now — *new young film star and director in public row . . .* '

'Where are we going?' she asked breathlessly as he propelled her along the narrow pavements bordering the canals.

'To my hotel. At least we'll get some privacy there.'

They sped over the shiny green waters of the Canal Giudecca in a lively motor launch, ending up at the landing stage of a traditional Venetian hotel, dignified and less lavish than the place Adam had booked for Zara.

Rick's room overlooked the sea. It was simple and uncluttered apart from a much-used copy of the film script and a pile of CDs with recordings of music from the sixteenth century.

Zara sat on a small carved chair beside the window watching the motor-boats race up and down on the waters of the canal below and the seagulls flying in from the lagoon dipping and diving then alighting on the tiled chimneys of the ancient buildings opposite. She envied them their free-dom of movement and action.

Rick leaned up against the wall, his hands tucked in the pockets of his jeans. 'I'm waiting,' he said quietly.

'I want to come off the film,' she said.

He shot her a burning glance. 'You want to quit?'

'Yes.'

There was a long silence. Zara could hear him breathing.

'I don't believe you,' he countered calmly.

'I want to be . . . out of it . . . it's not for me . . . '

'What's not for you? You seem to have taken to film acting like a duck to water. So what else is bothering you?'

'It's the publicity,' she said hastily. 'It's getting to me, making me nervous and panicky.'

His eyes sharpened. 'So panicky you've signed up to model swimwear in some very public locations? That doesn't seem to square up with a dislike for being in the limelight. Adam tells me that you're really keen.' She bowed her head. 'Don't lie to me, Zara,' he said in a low voice. 'It's not worthy of you, or me for that matter. Just tell me about the trouble you're in and I'll move heaven and earth to help.'

She sat as still and white as marble, having no strength left to continue deceiving him. He had moved to stand close beside her. He raised her very gently to her feet, his touch so tender that she longed for the caress to continue. 'Temptress,' he whispered. Zara stiffened. 'That was Harry Salt's description; 'A raven-haired temptress'. It was his catch-phrase for you when we discussed the casting. I almost resigned on the spot.'

'Is that how you think of me?' She tried to free herself from his grasp.

'No. Temptress implies calculation, manipulation and the ability to make people do wicked things against their will. You are not like that, Zara. You are simple and honest and down-to-earth.'

He held her firmly against him, his free hand stroking her hair. 'I shouldn't be doing this, but I don't know how else to make contact with you. Where is the girl who was so frank and open yesterday? The girl who acted like an angel but had her feet firmly on the ground?'

Tears stung her eyelids and she tried so hard to swallow them back. 'Please Rick, I should go now. We mustn't start getting involved like this.'

'No, maybe not.' But his arms remained tightly wrapped around her. ' "Who ever loved, that loved not at first sight?" ' he quoted, his eyes shining with self-mockery.

She had no resistance left. She melted into him and a silence fell over the room as they shared a deep and intimate kiss. Moments passed and then very slowly he released her.

'Oh, Rick,' she murmured.

'Well, at least that was real,' he commented dryly. 'You're damn good at acting, but that kiss was the genuine article. Now can I please ask for a similar degree of honesty about your feelings towards your work?' She sighed and turned her head away from him. 'When I looked into your face on the set this morning, I could tell you'd lost confidence in yourself, almost as if you were despising what you were doing. I was already wondering what to do about the fact that I was so attracted to you and I had hoped we could keep personal feelings aside until the end of filming. But when I saw you looking so disillusioned and miserable I wanted to find a way to let you know how much you are valued on the set . . . especially by me. And sometimes, actions speak louder than words.'

Zara felt her heart beating with love for him and for a moment her trust in Rick was such that she almost dropped her guard and told him everything. But then a picture of Wallis Bond's face filled her mind and reminded her of the damage that woman was prepared to do in order to get her own way.

Rick was watching her closely. 'Tell me what you're afraid of.'

She felt her features harden, firming up like setting plaster. 'Nothing,' she stated briskly. 'I'm tired because of my late night. And being a novice on the set is pretty tough.'

'Is someone threatening you?' he cut in.

'No.' Well, it wasn't a complete lie, was it? The main target of Wallis's threats was her father.

Rick's forehead creased in a heavy frown. 'Take the rest of the day off,' he said tersely. 'You're in no fit state to turn in a good performance. Go back to your hotel, chill out and then get a good night's rest. Tomorrow is another day.'

He guided her to the lift and offered a brief farewell. As she rode downwards the bitter taste of what she had been forced to do welled up afresh in a wave of revulsion and regret.

Arriving back at her own hotel she found that a note had been handed in for her. She knew it would be from Wallis and her head swam with dizzy fear as she opened it . . .

Your father has had a little accident. Not serious — this time. W.

She ran up to her suite, feeling sick

with apprehension and indecision. She knew she had to do something, and fast. She dialled Adam's number.

'I need to see you,' she cried the instant he answered. 'There's something I need to discuss straight away.'

'That's a bit tricky; I'm just about to set off to fly to Milan.'

'You have to cancel it. I need to see you in person. Urgently!'

Adam had never heard her like this before. He was at the door of her suite in twenty minutes flat. What he saw when she opened it shocked him.

'Good grief, Zara! Are you ill?' He gazed in horror at the haggard appearance of his most promising client. Her face was dead white and there was a strangely hunted expression in her eyes. Her features were stretched in lines of misery.

She shook her head, then handed him an envelope she had been clutching in her fingers.

He tore it open and unfolded the sheet inside. On it was written a brief and formal letter of resignation. Internally, Adam sighed. He had more than a little experience in dealing with prima donnas. 'Zara,' he said in the patient voice that kind teachers use to little children, 'What is this all about?'

'It's not a joke,' she said stiffly. 'It's totally serious.'

'Has someone on the set been getting under your skin, done something to upset you?' he asked calmly, then frowned, considering. 'Is Rick Crane the problem? I've known him reduce members of his cast to tears from time to time. Men as well as women.'

'Rick couldn't have been kinder,' Zara countered warmly. Adam stared at her in perplexity. 'I just can't stand any more of it,' Zara said in a low and desperate voice.

'Can't stand what for goodness sake?' Adam was struggling to maintain his customary relaxed demeanour.

'Being a star, always in the public eye . . . all that kind of thing . . . ' she finished lamely, knowing there was nothing worse she could have said to her manager and publicist.

Adam grappled manfully with this body blow. 'Zara, everyone in films and TV feels like that from time to time. There's this terrible anxiety about being public property, about one's personal space being eaten up. It's a perfectly normal feeling — and it will pass.'

Her hand trembled violently as she put it up to her forehead. 'I don't want to discuss it, Adam. I just want to get out.'

Adam did some rapid thinking. 'Do you remember the day we signed the contract?' he asked, cunningly inviting her to re-live those magical moments when both of them had realised that their whole future lives could be totally transformed. 'Harry Salt was captivated by you. He looked at you as though you were a queen. I think you could have asked him for the world on a plate and he wouldn't have been able to refuse you.'

Oh yes, Zara remembered, all right. It had been like a dream; she and Adam had flown out to Harry Salt's Los Angeles mansion for breakfast with the great man: a full English breakfast which he had laid on especially for them. She'd been so excited, she'd only managed to nibble a little toast.

Harry had clearly adored her on first sight. He was no fool, of course, and he had run a check on her previous acting form and demanded a screen test at one of his own studios before the contract was drawn up. But he was pretty sure she had a great future ahead of her.

After breakfast they had gone into his oak-panelled study and signed a contract which involved a huge advance payment and future payments of thousands of pounds. Zara had been elated and bemused when she realised that she and her father would most likely be free of financial worries for the rest of their lives. It had been hard to believe it. It still was.

'You bewitched him,' Adam commented. 'Just as you're going to bewitch millions of cinema goers when this film is released.'

'You make me sound like a magician, casting spells over people,' she murmured shyly.

'Yes, that's exactly what you are,' Adam replied smoothly. 'That is exactly what the film industry aims to do. It's a huge factory creating fantasies to make the humdrum of daily life less dreary.'

'Well, it's not right for me,' she reiterated stubbornly. 'I can't stand any more of it and I want you to give this letter to Harry and explain why I can't finish the film.'

'I can't very well explain things to Harry when I don't understand them myself,' Adam said sharply. 'You're not exactly talking sense, Zara.' There was a long, uneasy silence. 'Are you sure you haven't had a spat with Rick Crane?' Adam wondered. A flush crept up Zara's face. Suddenly Adam smiled. 'Have you fallen in love with him?

Come on Zara, admit it!'

'No!' Her face felt as it were giving off heat like an electric fire.

Adam chuckled. 'That's one of the major hazards of film-making, you know, falling under the magic of the director.'

'Can we please leave Rick out of this discussion, Adam? I'm utterly serious about wanting to come off the film.' She took in a deep breath and straightened her shoulders. 'It's for family reasons. I've got to go back to England to be with my father.'

'Why didn't you say that in the first place?' Adam countered.

'I should have. I'm very worried about him. I'm not thinking clearly.'

'Okay,' Adam said reasonably. 'Take a flight now. Go and reassure yourself he's all right. Hold his hand for a bit — and be back here tomorrow.'

She stood up, her eyes full of fire. 'No! I'm not coming back. Let someone else have the part.'

Adam's face hardened. 'You really do mean this, don't you? Have you any idea what you're asking? You can't just walk out of this film.'

'Why not?'

'If you walk out you'll have to pay back all the money you've been advanced plus a sizable indemnity payment to Salt's production company.'

Zara had a vague recollection of having seen this clause in the contract's small print. She had paid little attention to it. The idea of quitting hadn't so much as entered her thoughts on that carefree day.

'Film magnates aren't fools, Zara. They protect their interests very fiercely. You won't be the first star to storm out of a film on an emotional whim.' Adam's eyes had taken on a calculating and flinty quality. He was not going to give her one iota of support on this matter.

'I've no money besides the fees Harry paid me,' she whispered, her face white with panic. 'And I've already used some of that. I'd be bankrupt if I had to pay him back . . . '

Adam remained still and silent. He

looked like a man whose bones are made of steel. Zara had never seen him like this before. She felt almost frightened of him. She bit down hard on her lip.

Adam sensed he had played a trump card and achieved some success. He could afford to be a little more accommodating. 'Has your father taken a turn for the worse? I could get someone down there to the hospital to check things out for you.'

'He had a fall just this morning,' she said in a dull, flat voice. 'He sounded confused.' She had made contact with her father minutes after summoning Adam. The fragility in his voice had struck bleak terror into her.

'Well, that's to be expected after a fall. He's not critically ill, is he?'

'No. I don't think so.'

'Zara,' said Adam in his most persuasive tones. 'I do understand how you feel. But you can't throw up a leading part in a film just because your father has had a fall.'

118

Zara felt a stab of bitter anger. 'I can't come off the film full stop, can I? Not without ruining myself financially.'

'No, I'm afraid you can't.'

Her shoulders slumped, the fight all gone out of her.

Adam took her hand in his. 'I know you're going to be sensible,' he said in cajoling tones. 'Of course you mustn't dream of bankrupting yourself. Tomorrow you'll feel so much better. You'll be there on the set making everyone sit up and take notice. You're turning into a very fine actress, Zara. I don't want to hear one more word about throwing all this talent away.' He held his breath, waiting.

'No,' she whispered, feeling as if all routes of escape were being blocked off, one by one.

'Shall I stay in Venice for a day or two?' Adam offered gallantly. 'Would that make you feel better?'

'Thank you, Adam. There's no need for you to alter your programme. I'll be all right.'

Relief spread over Adam's face. 'And you'll be on the set tomorrow?'

Zara fought back the now familiar, grim feeling of being impossibly trapped. 'Yes, I'll be there, Adam.'

'Splendid.' At the door, just before leaving, Adam gave her a knowing smile. She smiled bravely back, knowing perfectly well that Adam was convinced he had been sorting out the results of some kind of love-tangle crisis. He thought his beautiful client had fallen foul of one of Cupid's capricious arrows. And as far as Adam was concerned, the man who was number one suspect in the case was undoubtedly Rick Crane. Well, let Adam think what he liked, Zara decided. It was neither here nor there what he thought on that score.

Later on, lying sleepless in bed, it struck her that there were only two people in the world whose personal opinion truly mattered to her, that of her father and that of Rick Crane. She went over and over her interview with

Rick, still amazed that his reactions to the manifestations of her dilemma had been so considerate and measured. Even after she had got to know him a little better, she would have predicted that he would have been wild with anger at her behaviour. She knew how important the film was to him and how he guarded the notion of professionalism as opposed to that of fame.

Through her recent behaviour she had shown herself to him as someone who was unreliable, petty, unco-operative and secretive. Exactly the sort of woman he despised and avoided. And yet he had not reacted with hardness or anger — quite the reverse — he had been patient and sensitive and truly kind. He had given her chance after chance to put things right. He had shown a readiness to persist in believing that there was some genuine and forgivable motive underlying her behaviour. Moreover, his shrewdness and depth of perception had led him close to guessing the truth.

Whilst Adam, in stark contrast, had

shown himself as a man who was quick to jump to superficial conclusions and who had no qualms about taking a tough and hard-faced approach. He was pleasant enough, outwardly polite and courteous, but he was someone whose mind was occupied with the making of money rather than the seeking of truth.

You live and learn, she concluded grimly. And she seemed to be learning pretty fast at the moment.

Rick's embrace had unnerved her, flooding her with new and bewildering feelings. She realised how much she wanted him: to be near him and hear the sound of his voice, share her innermost thoughts and feelings with him.

She longed for him to put his arms around her again, and for a moment her need for fulfilment with Rick almost transcended the paralysing anxiety about her father.

And now, ironically, to make things even worse, it seemed to her Rick's feelings were as intense as hers. He had as good as told her that he had been strongly attracted to her on their first meeting.

She briefly wondered if that had been the real reason for his initial hostility — anger with himself for being tempted by Harry Salt's hot new star?

The hours crept by and eventually the dawn began to paint itself across the sky in tentacles of pearly light stretching up from the horizon and over the lagoon, white trails of cloud appearing like feathers. In time the trails all vanished and the sky took on a glowing duck-egg blue shimmer.

But soon the dawn magic faded, and the day of harsh reality took over. A day that would surely be the worst of her life.

6

The sun was high over the Palazzo Ceccini as Zara approached its waterside
entrance. This morning she was more
than very late, she was spectacularly
late. She had reached the conclusion
that the only way to preserve her father's
safety and also avoid financial ruin was
to get herself thrown off the set and
declared psychologically unfit to go on
working.

She must act her heart out to appear
not only incompetent, but slightly
crazy. And she must do it fast. Given
the way she felt at the moment, this did
not seem too daunting a task. The solid
ground of her usually even tempera-
ment and balanced personality seemed
to be shifting beneath her feet like
grains of sand.

Up on the first floor of the palazzo
there was a buzz of conversation from

the cast and a good deal of action from the camera crew. Now in full costume and jewels, Zara lifted her hooped skirts over her knees to avoid the trailing electrical cables that snaked along the floor. She followed their winding path to discover what was going on.

Benny was the first person she saw, crouched by the small door that led into the tower she and Rick had climbed on the initial day of filming. He was swearing softly under his breath and looked up as she appeared, still wrestling with a length of cable and rather red in the face. She could see that beyond him the rest of his crew were proceeding laboriously up the steps with a burden of cameras, supports and other photographic para-phernalia.

'Hello beautiful,' he said. 'I was beginning to think you'd left us forever.'

'Oh, what do you mean?' Zara queried, attempting to look vague and not quite 'all there'.

'It's eleven o'clock,' Benny replied

dryly, returning to his wrestling task.

'Yes, I know.' She gave a trilling laugh and a little shrug. Benny looked up at her curiously. 'What are you doing?' she asked him, as though she had all the time in the world to chat, as though her mind was not in fact humming with apprehension at what would happen when Rick appeared.

'Trying to get enough equipment up this damned narrow stairway so we can do some shooting up there. Rick wants to explore the possibility of some shots from somewhere right at the top.'

A tingling chill ran down her body at the recollection of the awesome height of the tiny door overlooking the canal.

'I hope we're getting danger money,' Benny quipped cheerily. 'It won't exactly be a cameraman's dream working up there.'

'No,' she agreed in a carefree sing-song voice.

Footsteps were approaching, the steps of someone with a long and purposeful stride. Zara knew beyond a

126

doubt that it was Rick and felt her heart speed up like a sports car with the accelerator jammed on hard. Desperately she attempted to compose herself. Her palms had become hot and sticky and her mouth so dry she was convinced she would be unable to utter a word. Her body was quivering so much she thought she might literally black out and collapse on the floor.

White and trembling, she forced herself to face him.

'Good morning.' His voice was soft and intense and his hazel eyes as sharp and piercing as ever. Each time she met him she was struck afresh by their penetrating quality.

'Good morning,' she returned, feeling her throat close chokingly over the words, almost blocking their exit.

Rick said nothing further. He just waited . . . waited and watched.

This was horribly unnerving for Zara. She had expected anger or coldness, or maybe the assumed indifference of the day before. She had planned her personal script around one of those reactions — and now he was leaving her stranded and not knowing how to proceed. Seconds passed that seemed like hours. It was impossible to read his thoughts, for both his face and body were perfectly still and gave nothing away. All she could be sure of was that he was not burning with anger, she could see that he was far too composed for that.

Oh Rick! she thought. *I wish you would be angry, I wish you could give me some clue as to what you're thinking. Some straw to clutch at.*

'It's such a lovely morning, I went for a sail,' she said in her newly adopted fluty voice. 'Did anyone miss me?'

Rick tilted his head slightly. His lips gave the merest hint of a twitch. 'No, we didn't miss you at all. We shot one of the scenes where your presence is not required.'

Benny gave a low whistle. Clearly he was thunderstruck to see his longtime colleague behaving with such restraint and clemency in these intensely trying circumstances.

Zara stared up at Rick, attempting to appear befuddled.

'I had a word with Adam Leslie last night,' Rick told her. 'Adam of the silken tongue, your manager and spin doctor — he was revolving like a top.'

'Oh!' she said with a nonchalant little shrug as if to say, *So what?*

'He indicated that you were a bit 'under the weather' and you might be a little late this morning. So I didn't send out a search party, and of course I had every confidence you wouldn't desert us in our hour of need!' He raised an eyebrow in an ironic challenge. Zara closed her eyes for a second. He was teasing her in his sardonic way. And he was being so nice.

'Well, are you ready for some action?' Rick enquired.

'Yes, I'm ready,' she told him in her new frail and distant voice.

Rick walked with her down the corridor to the grand salon. He put his arm gently around her shoulders, making her shiver with delight despite all her efforts to block out the magic effect he had on her.

'Did you ever see Dame Maggie Dench playing Ophelia in Hamlet?' he asked her in conversational tones.

'Er, yes. I saw it on TV a year or two ago,' Zara said, puzzled.

'She played it rather like you're playing it now. Especially the 'mad' bits. Poor pining Ophelia becoming totally unhinged for love . . . ' His voice was a low, velvety growl.

Zara stiffened with indignation, recalling the passionate scene in his hotel room the day before. 'That's a rotten joke to make!' she burst out hotly. 'How could you be so callous?'

'I'm not in the least callous, Zara, just interested enough to know what's going on.' He looked down at her, concern and exasperation on his face. 'It's not cutting any ice with me. You can't pull the wool over my eyes by acting the part of the madwoman.'

'I must be a pretty useless actress, then,' she concluded bitterly.

'You're potentially a very fine actress,' he countered. 'But still raw, needing a lot more experience to round you out. I've been working in this scene for a very long time, and I know when someone is desperate rather than loopy.' He shot her a quizzical look. 'If you get my drift?'

She would not answer him. No way could she risk finally giving the whole game away. She had been a complete and utter fool. She should have known that a man of Rick Crane's perception would not be taken in by some ham acting motivated by personal desperation. What on earth was she going to do now?

They had reached the main salon and were ready to shoot the next scene. The young actor who was to play Zara's screen suitor was lounging on an ornate brocade-upholstered sofa reading a novel on his e-reader. He was quite remarkably good looking, with jet black hair, grey-green eyes and a strongly muscled body. He looked up expectantly as Rick and Zara came up to him. Even as a novice herself, she could see that he was dreadfully nervous, and her heart went out to him.

Rick's arm tightened under hers. He bent his head and whispered in her ear. 'I know better than to badger you into letting me in to your secret. But now that you're here, and you're reasonably sane, would you do me a favour and let me have a performance that bears some resemblance to the unlucky young Countess?'

Zara swallowed then walked up to her young co-star and smiled at him. He looked no more than sixteen. She supposed that was consistent with the original story which described the tender attraction the captive Countess had developed for the young man who helped look after the horses in her husband's stable. Supposed adultery with the young groom followed with the Countess becoming pregnant, thus ruining her chances of being swapped for the virgin Princess Elizabeth of England, and had stirred such a frenzy of rage in the Count, he had determined to be rid of his wife forthwith.

As usual before the scene was shot, Rick told its story to the cast and crew in his low-key yet spell-binding way. As was customary also, Zara found herself rapidly falling under the spell of his voice and narrative skill, filling up with a rush of inspiration which would enable her to act the part as though she were in fact the heroine in question.

But this morning, at the point where she felt herself drifting away into the past under the influence of Rick's story telling, she made a huge effort and jerked herself mentally back to reality like a dreamer springing from sleep when the dream becomes too threatening.

A few hours previously, as she had waited for the time to come when she could punch in the number of her father's hospital, Wallis had called her.

She had warned that today was Zara's very last chance, that if she did not get herself thrown off the set once and for all, well, she knew what to expect.

Reminding herself of that cryptic message Zara pushed all thoughts of Rick Crane to the very back of her mind. She sat beside the young actor and behaved with as much feeling as a log of wood; even the tone of her voice and the delivery of her words had a wooden feel to them.

Rick kept calling 'cut', making fresh explanations and demanding a fresh start. The nightmare went on like that for what seemed like years, yet Rick's patience seemed endless as Zara's despair escalated.

Then, at last, he was provoked.

In her role as the love-starved Countess, Zara was required to embrace the young groom, firstly with tenderness and then with growing urgency. Time and time again she folded her arms around him with limp disinterest and stretched a look of weariness and boredom over her features.

The unfortunate young actor looked helpless and humiliated. As Rick came striding up, he glanced at him in appeal. Rick gave him a sympathetic and approving nod, then sat down beside Zara, grasped her firmly by her upper arms and shook her — not with roughness but with a firmness that made her gasp in astonishment and colour leap into her face.

'Zara, what the hell are you playing at?' he demanded in a tight voice of fury. 'You're displaying about as much seductiveness as a floor mop!'

She turned her head away — it was too painful to look into his face. But he put his fingers around her jaw and pulled her back again to face him. 'You know damn well how to be seductive. And you know damn well how to kiss,' he growled. 'That, at any rate, I know for sure.'

She was suddenly aware that his head was lowering and his lips were moving close to hers. She watched in horrified fascination. Surely he was not going to give a demonstration of what he meant — not here, in front of all these people?

She attempted to wriggle out of his grasp but he had anticipated the move and had an iron grip on her. His lips were firm and insistent, yet warm and enquiring. He was irresistibly kissable and she was not able to hold out against him for more than a few seconds. She found her hands moving up around his neck and then her tongue was pressing between his lips, hungry for the taste of him. All sense of time and place were lost and when eventually they pulled away from each other Zara was startled to hear a gentle clip-clop of applause from the fascinated spectators.

Rick raised an eyebrow and gave a complicated little smile. 'That's what I'm after — got it?'

Before she could make any protest he had walked away and was making preparations for the filming to re-commence.

Zara felt as though she had been shattered into small particles. She experienced a painful bombardment of internal chaos and confusion, and it struck her suddenly that she was as much a captive of fate as the helpless Countess she was portraying.

As the young actor sat down beside her once again, she turned to him and said, 'I'm sorry, I can't go on with this. It's nothing to do with you, please believe me.' Tears almost choking her, she picked up her skirts and fled from the room.

Her high wooden clogs clanged against the stone floors as she ran down the corridor, gathering speed. She shook them off in exasperation, kicking them aside, hearing them land with a clattering thud on the stonework. Then she pulled off the constricting red wig and flung it away to join the clogs.

She was simply running now, on automatic pilot, having no clear goal or purpose. She found herself following the camera cables which led to the door of the tower. At the entrance she caught the sweet smell of fresh air, the tang of the sea; the tiny door at the top must have been opened. She hitched her skirts high over her arms and climbed the narrow steps, plunging into a darkness that gradually brightened as the light from the high slit-like windows penetrated down.

There was just one member of the camera crew technicians at the top, working on cable connections. The main crew were still in the big salon.

'Hi.' He smiled, curious, but used to seeing all sorts in this line of work. It did strike him that the leading lady had a wild, dream-like look on her face.

'Can I get through to look at the view, please?' Zara asked distractedly.

'Sure.' He flattened himself against the wall to let her pass. There was barely room for him and her and all the hoops of the farthingale. The little door hung wide open. Zara drew in a sharp breath. The height and the breadth and the beauty she saw were incredible.

Venice! City of boats and gulls, of churches and lapping canals, of narrow passageways and stray cats. A watery apparition under a golden autumn sky. She could see the bright sails of the yachts and the flashing waters of the Lagoon in the distance. And closer to, the ancient and crumbling walls of the Palazzo Ceccini, the reflections wobbling precariously in the green waters of the canal below.

'Pretty fantastic, isn't it?' her companion commented. 'We certainly need to get some shots from here. Too good to miss.' He went on with his work, whistling softly to himself.

Zara climbed onto the sill, crouching in the doorway, her hands clinging to the rotting wooden edges. Dimly she was aware of voices below coming nearer. Her own head seemed to be filled with voices: her father's, at first cheery then frail and confused; Adam's, smooth but so coolly manipulative; Wallis's metallic and wicked; and Rick's

— vibrant and vital and deep with understanding. Fate had decreed that she was not able to respond meaningfully to any of these voices. She was worn out with wrestling with the problem of how to do it.

The real-life voices were coming closer and closer. Her heart beat thickly. She did not think that she could face another confrontation; no matter who it was with. She began to feel a curious sense of lightness, as though she were weightless and transparent. All anxiety seemed suddenly to have left her as her escape route became apparent.

Quite calmly she loosened her grasp on the edges of the door frame and allowed the weight of her body to be propelled forwards slightly. All that was required now was a very gentle push against the wall with her feet to alter the balance of her weight so that more of it was outside the door than in.

Gently and very smoothly she became airborne; her body moving over the glinting green waters of the canal, free and unanchored. She began her descent, her skirts billowing out, her dark hair streaming in the wind.

★　★　★

Rick took the steps three at a time, but by the time he reached the little sill beyond the door Zara was already in the water, her huge skirts swirling around her like sails. Startled tourists were watching the scene in fascination, some of them taking pictures on their mobile phones.

'Get her out!' Rick bellowed down in fury. 'Someone get her out!'

Pushing past the open-mouthed camera crew technician, he began to make his way back down the steps, wanting to be with Zara as soon as possible. Suddenly he turned. 'Did she say anything?' he demanded of the technician. 'Before she jumped?'

The man shook his head. 'No. She just seemed in a kind of . . . trance.'

141

'Hellfire!' Rick raced down to the corridor, knowing it would take a minute or so for him to reach the place Zara had fallen. He would have to go through the garden to get onto the pavement edge of the small canal.

By the time he reached the spot he saw that Zara had been pulled to the side of the canal, but no one had been able to lift her from the water because of her being weighed down with her period costume. Without hesitation Rick leapt into the canal and heaved her from the green slimy water. Soon she was lying on the pavement with a small and curious crowd around her. A young man came to kneel beside her, feeling her pulse, gently lifting her closed eyelids and looking into her eyes. He seemed to be taking a cool and professional view of the incident.

Rick, dripping and panting, looked up from the white-faced Zara. 'Are you a doctor?' he asked the man, praying he could speak English.

He turned. 'I'm a medical student,'

he said. 'She's breathing rather slowly, and her pulse is erratic.'

'We need to get her to the hospital,' Rick said. The young medic agreed.

An ambulance had already been called and a big covered motor launch was coming up the canal. Men with a stretcher and blankets rushed forward. Rick spoke to them in Italian and they eventually allowed him to carry her very gently into the boat. Rick cradled her limp body in his arms, not wasting time regretting what had happened, simply praying that she was going to make a full recovery.

The film could blow up in smoke for all he cared. He just needed Zara to be well again, to find out what had driven her to such a desperate action, and then help her to put things right. He never took his eyes from her as the boat's siren wailed and the engine revved up allowing them to speed over the little back canal before turning into the Canal Giudecca.

He looked down at her pale face.

Fate was so capricious and life was so fragile, he thought, willing this young woman with whom he had fallen in love to hold on to its slender thread.

★ ★ ★

Pictures were swirling in her mind. Shapes and colours and lights were shining behind her eyes. There was the sound of an engine throbbing.

Gradually things came into focus. In the background she saw pulsing blue flashes . . . a brilliant silver sun . . . in the foreground something grey . . . grey overlaid with fine black and white stripes . . . a shirt . . . Rick's shirt.

She put up a hand and touched the fabric tentatively. She felt herself clasped firmly in his arms, in no way restrained, but blissfully held and protected. There was no longer any need to go on thrashing in futile despair.

'You're soaking wet,' she said in a frail, puzzled voice.

'So are you,' he said softly. 'One of the hazards of wallowing in a canal.'

Memory was returning. She felt appalled when she thought of what she had done. Shamed and guilty too.

He was stroking her hair with long, slow sweeps of his hand. She sighed and leaned her body close against him. She could hear his heart thudding violently beneath her ear. He too must be very shocked, she realised.

'I know there's a quest for reality in the acting profession, but that was taking it a bit too far,' he quipped dryly, even though still reeling from the shock of her astonishing jump from the tower.

Images filtered into Zara's mind as she began to re-live those last few seconds in the tower. She had not planned to jump, nor had she launched herself into the air in a last ditch attempt to rid herself of despair and frustration. Not consciously anyway; she had simply felt herself to be temporarily weightless both in body and spirit.

'I didn't mean to do it,' she murmured softly to Rick. 'I didn't plan it.' She closed her eyes in horror at what she had risked when she let herself fall from the little door.

'Hush, it's okay, I understand. Don't try to talk.' He went on rocking her against him as though she were an injured child.

'I'm so sorry,' she persisted. She pictured how her spectacular fall must have appeared both to Rick and the passing pedestrians. She had caused nothing but grief and trouble.

'You could have been seriously hurt,' he agreed. 'Killed, even.' His heartbeat faltered. 'My God, I would never have forgiven myself . . . '

'But it wasn't your fault . . . ' Suddenly she had become focused, knowing she couldn't deceive him for a moment longer — she had to trust him.

Before she could speak, he asked her softly, 'Whose fault was it? Who's been blackmailing you?'

She took his hands in hers and

grasped them tightly. 'Wallis Bond . . . '
Then panic filled her eyes and she
pleaded, 'You mustn't tell anyone, not a
soul! She'll hurt my father, perhaps
even kill him.'

He stared at her in dismay then let
out a long breath of astonishment and
touched her cheek gently. 'Of course I
won't; you have my word.'

They sat in silence for a few
moments. Zara felt herself drawing
strength from his calm presence and his
quiet authority. Suddenly she wanted to
tell him everything, every little detail of
Wallis's threats and torments.

The words poured out as he listened
with growing horror, his features still
and reflective throughout.

She longed to know what he was
thinking, but he said nothing more. She
began to shiver, the shock and the
coldness biting into her. She saw that
Rick's face was white and chilled too.
'I'm so sorry,' she whispered again.

He held her close. 'You've certainly
given me some food for thought with

147

your bombshell about Wallis.'

She stiffened. 'Oh no, I wish I hadn't told you.'

'You should have told me right from the start. And if you weren't suffering from the after-effects of an accident, I'd be giving you hell about being so independent and stubborn.'

'I was paralysed with fear. My brain just wouldn't work properly.'

'Okay, Okay.' He smiled. 'Just be quiet now and try to stay calm. If the medics find that your vital signs are all normal, that will be reassuring. But it's possible you might be admitted for a period of observation.' She groaned. 'There's no need to worry,' he said. 'We'll sort out the nasty problem of Wallis Bond later.' He made it sound as though there might actually be a solution to be found.

At the hospital she underwent a careful check from the cheerful Venetian medical staff. They communicated with each other in a mixture of their patchy English and Zara's sparse

Italian, and to her great relief their tests showed that she had sustained no serious injuries. Eventually she was given a clean bill of health and told to go home, take things easy for a few days.

Rick, who had stayed close beside her whenever possible, grinned and murmured, 'You'll be lucky. We've got work to do and a film to make.'

Zara glanced at him. He clearly had something in mind regarding the Wallis issue. He would have been mulling it over and must have come to some kind of solution, even in this short time. But how could that be? she wondered after her brief euphoria had passed. Rick may be the most fantastic man on earth as far as she was concerned; but even he might have difficulty getting to grips with the machinations of a woman as demonically driven as Wallis Bond.

'You should stop frowning, Zara,' Rick said in wry tones. 'You're about to be on camera. The price of fame,' Rick smiled. 'Are you up to it, or shall I get rid of them?'

Zara saw that the paparazzi were out in force at the main entrance to the hospital and a little group of medical staff had gathered in the foyer in the hope of getting her autograph. Dutifully Zara signed her name for the staff who had given her such attentive care. The paparazzi she could have done without, although she was beginning to realise that putting up with their shrill and hysterical interest was part of her job.

Her job! Did she still have a job? She suddenly felt uncertain once again.

Rick came up behind her. 'Go out there and wow them all,' he said. 'You're Zara Silk, young and lovely and on the way to becoming a fine actress. And you're certainly not a girl to be intimidated by hysterical harpies like Wallis Bond.' He raised an eyebrow in that quizzical manner she was coming to know and love so well. 'Are you hearing me, Miss Silk?'

'I'm hearing you,' she replied with a

smile, feeling her heart fluttering over his words of encouragement.

'Right. Out you go then and give them the works. We want Harry Salt to be proud of you.'

Zara could not imagine what he was cooking up, but she was convinced it was a scheme to be reckoned with. She smiled confidently as flash bulbs fizzed and popped.

'Meez Seelk, you are not injured?' a man asked, waving his camera.

'I'm fine, absolutely fine.' Feeling the wildness of her hair around her face and looking down at her crumpled costume, she gave a rueful smile as she wondered what kind of pictures would emerge.

'Eez it not dangerous to do your own stunts?' the photographer persisted, admiration in his eyes.

Do her own stunts? It took her a moment to understand what he was getting at. Clearly some people, seeing the shots which had been taken at the scene must have assumed she was doing a stunt for the film.

'Oh, there was little danger,' she said, with admirable composure. 'The canal is quite shallow at that point and we took every precaution.' *If they swallow that they'll swallow anything*, she thought.

A sudden and desperate weariness came over her. She just wanted to find a bolt hole where she could curl up and go to sleep. Preferably with Rick close by to ensure that her world did not run crazy again.

She heard his voice behind her. 'That's enough, guys,' he said firmly. 'Miss Silk needs to rest now.' He took her arm and propelled her forwards. The press corps parted like the Red Sea before Moses.

'Will you restart filming again tomorrow, Mr Crane?' a voice enquired.

'Miss Silk and I will resume filming as soon as possible,' Rick replied.

White with renewed fear, Zara thought she should take issue with Rick as they went back along the canal in a hired motor taxi. What was Wallis going to make of this morning's events, and of Rick's words to the press? Surely they would drive her to even more desperate acts.

As she struggled with her thoughts she felt her eyes closing and by the time they reached his hotel she was almost faint with exhaustion. 'There'll be more paparazzi waiting at your hotel,' he explained, as he helped her from the boat. 'You'll be better here.'

As they went into the quietness of his suite, the relief of being in a safe and private place was overwhelming, but her legs still felt wobbly and she had to put a hand out to steady herself as she staggered through the door. Without a word of warning Rick lifted her into his arms, carried her into the bedroom and laid her on the bed. She felt his hands begin to strip off the heavy, still damp brocade of her costume.

She wanted to stay awake. She wanted to be with him in mind and body, to place herself in his arms and show him how very much she cared for him.

Yet at the same time the need to sleep was washing over her like a great tidal wave and she felt herself falling into a soft velvety blackness.

But then suddenly, she thought of her father, and the danger he was still exposed to. 'Oh, Rick you shouldn't have given the press the idea we'd soon be filming again,' she told him. 'If Wallis gets even a sniff of suspicion that I'm going to be back on the set, and still the leading lady in the film, she'll go crazy.'

'Don't worry,' he told her, his face grim. 'Within the next few hours all sorts of things will have changed.' He dropped a light kiss on her cheek and then suddenly, he was through the door and gone. Once more she was alone and defenceless, her problems still tormenting her. She fell back against the pillows. The nightmare was beginning all over again.

7

Rick paced up and down the reception room of his suite, his mind humming with plans. Gradually a strategy began to form. He reached for his phone and made a number of calls, then went down to the reception lobby, planning to go out in search of Wallis at her hotel. But his journey wasn't necessary — she was just coming through the garden entrance to his hotel as he walked from the lift.

'Rick!' she exclaimed. Her eyes were sparkling with suppressed excitement. She walked up to him, almost matching his height in her Jimmy Choo skyscraper heels. She stretched up and kissed him on both cheeks, continental style. 'Mwoi, mwoi!' she purred.

Rick felt his senses come on red alert. He pushed her gently away. 'You and I need to have a talk, Wallis.'

She smiled. 'Indeed we do, darling. That's why I'm here.'

'Okay,' he said easily. 'Shall we go up to my suite?'

'Sure. A cosy little chat would be just the thing.'

As they rode the lift up to his floor, Wallis kept glancing at him with her flashing eyes. She really did have a very powerful presence, Rick thought, but there was an unmistakable hint of menace beneath her smiling façade. He wasn't at all surprised that she'd managed to get under Zara's skin with her crazy threats.

Rick settled her in a corner of the silk-upholstered sofa and offered her a drink. 'Champagne?' he suggested, pulling a bottle of fizz from the mini-bar.

'Perfect,' she said, crossing her long, slender legs. 'I feel in the mood for celebration today.'

He popped the cork, filled glasses and placed them on the low table.

Wallis took a sip. She was wearing a

zebra print dress made of some clinging material that draped around her hour-glass figure. Her gleaming blonde hair was loose and waving over her shoulders. A rope of small flashing diamonds dangled from each ear. She looked sensational — and was well aware of it.

She raised her glass. 'To us,' she said. 'And our future work together.' Her glossy lips curved in a fetching smile.

Rick narrowed his eyes. 'How so?'

'I'll be taking over Zara's part in the film,' she said sweetly. 'As from . . . well, now I suppose.'

Rick's heart beat like a steeple-chaser in the Grand National. This woman had an ego the size of a mountain. He schooled himself to stay calm. 'I think not,' he said evenly. 'But perhaps you'd like to tell me where you got that unlikely idea from?'

'From the boss, Rick darling, the top man,' she whispered seductively. 'Need I say more?'

'Are we talking about Harry Salt?'

'We are.' She paused to take a sip of

champagne. 'And I was talking to him earlier on a video link. I thought he had a right to know that filming has more or less been at a standstill for the past two days, and from what my friends in the business tell me, Zara has proved to be a bit of a disaster. She gets in late in the mornings, is very erratic with her acting performance, and to crown it all she seems positively unhinged. Whoever heard of a leading lady jumping out of a tower into a canal?'

Rick closed his eyes and made a superhuman effort to stop himself grabbing the gloating Wallis and shaking her smug expression from her face. He assumed an expression of gravity. 'So what has Harry decided?'

'Well, obviously, he was pretty upset to hear what had happened and so sorry for poor little Zara, but naturally he has to think of the film and how it's costing a fortune to have it held up. And I'm here in Venice!' She spread her arms in a gesture of gleeful triumph. 'I'm free to come on the set immediately, and of course I'll burn the midnight oil to learn the lines.'

'I see . . . ' he said.

'I simply loved the book about the Countess Ceccini and I've always wanted to portray her,' she cooed.

Rick gave her a long, level look; the kind of look that would have most people in the entertainment business quaking, and even Wallis appeared slightly disconcerted for a moment.

She soon recovered. 'I'm so right for the part,' she said. 'Even though I'm a little older than Zara, I've always looked after myself. I'm in great shape — better than a lot of women in their twenties.'

'I won't argue with that, but I can't agree to your standing in for Zara.'

'You'll have no choice,' she said. 'Harry will simply tell you what he has decided. What Harry wants he always gets, and he wants me for the part.'

'Not a chance,' Rick said with dangerous calm.

'It's decided,' she shot back. 'And

don't even think of trying to change Harry's mind. He doesn't do U-turns. You may not like it, but you'll just have to put up with it. After all you wouldn't want to resign from the film, would you, Rick?' Wallis continued. 'That would be professional suicide.'

'It would,' Rick agreed.

'I'm so glad you're not going to be difficult,' Wallis said, taking another sip of champagne. 'By the way, how is poor Zara — resting at her hotel?'

'No. She's here, resting in bed — right next door.'

'Really,' Wallis drawled. 'Well, I guess she'll have time to get a whole lot of rest in the near future.'

Rick stood up, reining in his growing rage. 'I'll just go check on her,' he said. 'Do help yourself to a top-up.'

In the bedroom he shook Zara gently to wake her. 'How are you feeling?'

She smiled sleepily at him. 'Better,' she said.

'Good. We have a visitor. Wallis.' She gave a low groan. 'She and I have been having a little chat and I think it would be a good idea if you were to come and join us.'

Zara struggled into a sitting position and ran her fingers through her hair, which was still damp and tangled. 'Has Wallis . . . done anything terrible?'

He shook his head. 'Trust me, Zara, everything is going to be all right, truly, but I need you to be there and listen to what Wallis has to say. And don't bat an eyelid, no matter what she comes out with. I have things well in hand, believe me.'

She took a moment to think. 'Okay then, I'll come. Give me time to wash my face and find a dressing gown.'

'There's one in the bathroom. Don't be long. I don't want Wallis prowling about on her own.'

Zara was ready in two minutes flat, standing at the door and surveying the woman who had caused her so much angst.

'Come and sit by me, sweetie,' Wallis said. 'How are you feeling?'

'Pretty good,' Zara said, sitting as far away from Wallis as possible.

'Shall I tell Zara my news?' Wallis asked Rick, arching an eyebrow.

'Go ahead.'

Zara felt her nerves give a sickening jerk, instantly thinking of her father and dreading to hear the worst.

Wallis smirked. 'You see Zara, because of your little accident today, you're going to need to rest up a bit, so I've had a word with Harry and he's given me the go-ahead to step into the part of the Countess.' She gave Zara a treacherous smile.

Zara's mouth fell open. She started to speak and then stopped herself. Her eyes swivelled to Rick. *Trust me*, he was telling her. She took a deep breath, dug down into her personal reserves and spoke with new conviction. 'Well, you finally got what you wanted, Wallis.'

The smile faded from Wallis's face, as she heard the quiet self-confidence in Zara's tone. Being an arch manipulator she had the ability to suss out what was going on beneath the surface of things and her senses were telling her that something here was not quite right. But then she reminded herself of her little video chat with Harry. All was well. She reinstated her smile.

'We'll talk more about the part later,' Rick said in even tones. 'Let's just talk for a while about your blackmailing exploits against Zara.'

Wallis's pupils dilated. 'Blackmail? Me? Don't be ridiculous!'

'Yes. Blackmail.'

Wallis glanced across to Zara, realising she had been letting Rick in on a few secrets. The stupid child!

'Well, perhaps I was a little out of line, but there was no real harm meant.' She re-crossed her legs and straightened her skirt. Her smile was becoming tight-lipped.

'No?' said Rick. 'Making threats about the safety of Zara's father. Telling her she had to be off the set as soon as possible to ensure that he was not harmed in some way.'

'I never made any specific threat,' Wallis said coldly.

'You didn't need to,' Zara said. 'You just kept insisting that the worst would happen if I didn't do exactly as you said.'

Wallis tried to brazen it out. 'I was just playing a little game with you . . . '

'No, it wasn't a game,' Zara insisted. 'You told me I was going to give up my role to you 'on a plate'. That you had people at the hospital watching my father. That I had to make such a hash of my acting I'd get myself thrown off the set. And that if I didn't manage to do that and let you step in to my shoes, then 'contingency plans had already been made' regarding my father. Do you deny it?' Zara had spoken without hesitation. Even though she was not sure just what was going on, her confidence was growing by the minute.

Wallis was beginning to look rattled. There was a significant pause.

'Because of your threats, Zara was driven to risk her life today,' Rick told

Wallis in a voice of ice. 'And you should be grateful she wasn't killed.'

'Oh, come on,' Wallis protested. 'That's being a bit melodramatic!'

'A thirty-foot drop into a shallow canal. She was miraculously lucky to hit a patch deep enough to absorb the impact, and if she had been badly injured or killed, Miss Wallis Bond, I would have made sure justice was done as far as your part in it was concerned.'

'Don't make me laugh, Rick. Not only did she jump of her own free will, that line on harassment and provocation never holds up in a court of law.'

'Oh, I wasn't talking about courts and tricky and expensive lawyers LA-style. I'm talking about simple and brutal matters like underhand blackmail.'

'Oh, yeah.' Wallis affected total indifference.

'I'd have made sure you were ruined forever both professionally and personally . . . ' Rick paused and watched Wallis's face turn ashen, then added,

'And I intend to do that anyway.'
Silence. 'Blackmail is very effective,' he
went on. 'As you found with Zara, and
no doubt with a number of unfortu-
nates before her who happened to get
in your way.'

Wallis's features took on an ugly
twist.

'You made me believe you really
would harm my father,' Zara said, then
for a moment her new-found confidence wavered. 'Is he okay?' she found
herself whispering.

'You're such a little innocent! Do you
really think I'd risk my skin for some
obscure old guy who's a hospital case?'

'You mean it was all just bluff?' Zara
burst out. 'No — I don't buy that. You
truly meant all the awful things you said
to me.'

'Oh sure, I've had people there at the
hospital. It was quite fun organising
that. And your dear daddy did have a
fall, but it was a genuine accident.
Nicely timed as far as I was concerned,
but simply an accident.'

Zara could not believe how horribly she had been tricked. How naïve she had been, how impressionable. 'What about the part in the film?' she demanded. 'You were deadly serious about that.'

'Oh, she wanted the part all right, didn't you, Wallis?' Rick was fixing her with his intense gaze, pinning her down like a butterfly to a display board.

For a moment Wallis looked alarmed. 'Look, I'm getting pretty sick of this,' she snapped at him, rallying. 'I've got what I wanted. Nobody's been maimed or killed. Now I'm going to leave.' She stood up.

'Sit down,' Rick said in a soft voice that nevertheless could have cleft stone. Wallis hesitated, then sat down again. Leisurely Rick stretched out his long legs. 'I'm going to tell you both a story.'

Wallis snorted with frustration. 'I thought we were all done here.'

'Don't worry, it's a short one, though not very sweet. Around twenty years ago a young actress called Lauren

167

Doncaster landed a star part in a film called *Catwalk Babes*. It was a sexy romp charting the private lives of top international models. Lauren became quite famous and very rich. Wherever she went on stage or in cabarets, the place was sold out. There was another blockbuster film called *Private Parties* and more cabaret work. And then things went sour for Lauren. A third film flopped, the offers tailed off and dwindled to nothing. Suddenly she was thirty-five and all washed up.' Rick paused, watching as Wallis become very still, her eyes narrowed and guarded.

'Then along came film magnate Harry Salt,' he continued. 'He saw potential in Lauren for making megabucks in one of the up and coming TV soaps. He landed her a queen bee part in one and took her to live with him in his Beverly Hills mansion — and they were very happy for a year or two.'

'You lousy — ' Wallis fumed, gritting her splendid array of teeth. 'I've heard just about enough.'

Rick shook his head. 'They were quite happy until Lauren began to get restless and ever more greedy. The soap storyline was becoming boring. And to crown everything, Lauren — or rather Wallis Bond as she was professionally known — could see her fortieth birthday looming up with alarming speed.'

Zara was astonished. She had never guessed Wallis was in her forties. She couldn't help sneaking an admiring glance at her.

'To add insult to injury, Harry was enthusiastically promoting a young unknown girl from England who'd been spotted by a canny publicist. She was young and fresh and natural — as well as genuinely talented. Harry was rather taken with her . . . '

'He was besotted!' Wallis broke in angrily. 'He's crazy about everything British — vintage Bentleys, paintings of sheep on dreary moors, the Royal Family, you name it. He looked at little Zara with her country shepherdess complexion and her big violet eyes and there was nothing he would refuse her. Even a part in a film that promised to be a winner with a world renowned director holding the reins. Zara Silk with her virginal expression and box-office body. He was going to make her the darling of the decade. And when Harry makes up his mind, things happen.'

'And you were wild with jealousy and determined to topple that girl from Harry's golden pedestal,' Rick added.

Wallis affected icy indifference. 'Pretty well on target, Rick. You do your research well and your guesswork isn't bad. But, so what — who is going to be the slightest bit interested?'

'Harry, of course,' Rick said patiently. 'Harry may be used to egocentric stars, but he's basically a moral kind of guy, and blackmail is a pretty immoral and nasty kind of crime. Especially of the cruel sort you've been inflicting on Zara. That would be way beyond Harry's comfort zone. I got to know quite a lot about Harry's views on life when we discussed the screenplay for the film.'

Wallis's eyes became glinting and wary.

'So I'm sure he would be very distressed to hear the details of your behaviour towards Zara,' Rick added.

'Your word against mine, darling,' Wallis said.'

'I have proof,' Rick said slowly. He got up, crossed to the desk which stood against the wall opposite to Wallis and picked up a tiny camcorder which was cleverly concealed between his complete Shakespeare and the film script. He laid it on the low table in front of Wallis.

She closed her eyes.

He switched the recorder on and Wallis's voice sprang out, drawling and contemptuous, totally unrepentant regarding her treatment of Zara. And then Zara, so clear and precise, so eloquent. And all the beans were being spilled.

Wallis froze. 'So what are you going to do with your little discovery?' she demanded, desperately struggling to maintain her calm.

Rick smiled at her, saying nothing, letting her work it out for herself.

'You're not going to give this recording to Harry!' Colour drained from her face. 'You wouldn't do that — you wouldn't stoop to anything so low.'

Rick raised an ironic eyebrow. 'Wouldn't I?'

'Look, I didn't mean any harm and I'm real sorry now,' she begged, becoming desperate. 'I'll call off my people at the hospital right now.'

'You're unbelievable!' Zara broke in.

Wallis waved a dismissive hand at her and leaned forward towards Rick. 'Listen, I'll give you megabucks for that camera — just name your price.'

He shook his head and she saw that he was immovable.

'What are you going to do?' she asked in flat tones.

'Oh, I've already done plenty,' he said. 'A couple of hours back I spoke to the Chief Executive Officer at the hospital where Zara's father is being cared for. He's a friend of mine, by the way, a big supporter of the National Theatre. He was most concerned to hear there were intruders in his hospital. When we spoke again some time later they were already under arrest and being questioned by the police.'

Wallis's face was now blank and stony.

'Tampering with a hospital switchboard and posing as a doctor are illegal,' Rick pointed out.

'Cut the sermon,' Wallis snarled. 'What else?'

'I put a call through to Harry, who, strangely enough, was about to contact me. He was rather worried about the talk that you and he had earlier, and didn't think your story quite made sense. He was especially concerned for Zara's welfare and about the film being held up, naturally.'

'He told me I could have the part,' said Wallis, her voice petulant like a mutinous and spoilt child.

'He allowed you to think that,' Rick acknowledged. 'But only to give himself time to find out what has really been happening. At the end of our talk he told me to reassure Zara that she is still under contract in the leading part. He asked me to pass the message on to you.'

Wallis sat very still, staring down at her shoes.

'I got the feeling Harry doesn't trust you, Wallis.' Rick said softly. 'Maybe he hasn't done for some time . . . '

Wallis took in a long, slow breath. She threw her head back and tossed her hair. 'Oh well, some things don't go as you expect. You win some, you lose some. I guess I'm going to have to concede and make my exit.'

She uncurled herself from the sofa, flashed an evil smile first at Rick and then at Zara, and then, with a sudden and unexpected snake-like movement, she shot out her hand and snatched up the tiny camcorder from the table.

Zara jumped up in alarm as Wallis rushed it to the door and flung it open, the camera clutched tightly in her fist.

Just outside the doorway two uniformed officers from the Venice Questura were awaiting her. She gave a shriek, kicking and struggling as they halted her progress to take her into custody.

'Did I forget to mention that I called the police earlier?' Rick said wryly. 'Those so-called 'games' you played with Zara were the acts of a common criminal and now you're going to pay.'

Wallis bared her teeth at him, giving a very good portrayal of a dangerous tiger. She opened her hand, flung the mini camcorder to the floor and raised a stiletto heel to stamp on it. But Rick was too quick for her, swiftly scooping it up and handing it to one of the officers.

'Evidence,' he said.

Wallis finally capitulated and allowed

herself to be guided down the corridor. She walked erect, her head held high. Suddenly she turned, her raptor gaze homing in on Zara. 'Don't build up your hopes for a fairytale happy-ever-after with Rick Crane,' she said with honeyed sweetness. 'He has a bit of a reputation as a love-'em-and-leave-'em type. Check it out, darling. I'm telling you no lies.' She turned again and continued to walk on, flanked by the two officers. 'Ciao!' she called, giving a languid wave.

As Zara walked slowly back into the room, Rick placed his arm around her shoulders. 'She's gone,' he said. 'You've got your life back. Tomorrow is another day, as Scarlett O'Hara once remarked.'

She hardly heard his words, for she was still hearing Wallis's parting shot, and suddenly her new-found mood of confidence and optimism vanished.

8

The engines reached a roaring crescendo as the plane lifted off the Tarmac. Zara watched Venice sink down into the distance, a pin board of lights threaded with dark ribbons of water.

Rick sat beside her with half-closed eyes.

Zara struggled to put Wallis's hateful suggestions out of her mind and focus on something else. 'What will happen to Wallis?' she wondered aloud.

'I would think she'll be charged with both blackmail and initiating a scam to interfere with hospital procedure. Those are both Crown Court offences in the UK. Of course she'll hire a top-notch lawyer to defend her, but she'll almost definitely end up doing a stretch in prison.'

Zara was quiet for a time. 'Why did

Harry offer her my part?'

'He told me that he didn't really; he just gave her that impression by not arguing with her when she kept insisting that he should hand it to her. He couldn't think of any other way to get her off the video link. She was doing his head in — his words, not mine — and he'd been thinking about breaking things off with her for some time, apparently.'

'Oh, dear . . . '

Rick glanced down at Zara. 'You're not feeling sorry for her, are you?'

'No. But I wouldn't wish anyone any harm.'

'She's hard as nails and slippery as a lemon pip,' Rick said dryly. 'She'll get by, even if she has to rough it for a bit.' An air steward came by and offered them fresh coffee and croissants. 'I've never had star treatment on a private plane before,' Rick commented, taking a bite of the melting pastry.

'Because you're just a humble director,' Zara smiled.

He grinned. 'Too true! You're the new shining star and the great Harry Salt had to make sure his new star gets to see her dad so she can go back to work on his film in tip-top form.'

'Even if it meant sending his personal jet to collect her,' Zara remarked shyly. 'It was rather sweet of him.'

Rick laughed. 'Harry Salt's certainly a special sort of guy.'

They touched down at six am in a private airfield close to the hospital where Zara's father was being cared for, a car waiting to take them there.

Seeing the familiar little hospital, Zara felt suddenly choked up. 'What am I going to say to him?' she asked Rick. 'I hope he doesn't have a terrible shock when he sees me.'

'Just go in there and be the daughter he's always known,' Rick reassured her. 'I'll join you in a few minutes.'

Zara found her father in the same small ward he had been when she last saw him; he was looking happy and contented, reading the newspaper.

She walked in and perched on the edge of the mattress. 'Hello, Dad.'

He blinked with surprise. 'Zara!' Delight spread over his features as he hugged his daughter close, then he drew back and with a deeply concerned expression, said, 'Are you all right, love?'

She nodded, wondering why he looked so worried about her.

He picked up the paper and showed her the photograph on the front; a dramatic picture of a young woman flying through the air, hair streaming, huge crinoline skirts billowing. *Film star in daring stunt leap*, ran the caption. Her father gave a watery smile. 'Very realistic, but a bit risky wasn't it?'

Zara gave a neutral smile, trying to conceal her astonishment at this fresh slice of publicity.

'Well, I hope there won't be any repeat performances,' her father said. 'And what are you doing here, anyway?'

'Having a short break. I lost some of my concentration after I heard about

180

your fall. Rick Crane, my director suggested I fly back to England to make sure you're okay . . . he's here as well.'

Her father looked amazed. 'You certainly are living in a different world now,' he mused.

Rick slipped quietly in to the room to join them. Zara introduced them; the two most significant men in her life.

Rick enquired politely about her father's health. 'I hear you had a fall recently,' he commented.

'Oh, that was all my fault — trying to run before I could walk. Literally!'

Her father seemed in such good form that Zara felt huge relief. 'You mentioned a new doctor from the States who had been looking after you,' she commented.

'Yes, nice chap. He came to see me two or three times a day. An ace chess player; we had some good games and it certainly kept me busy and out of mischief for hours.'

Rick and Zara exchanged glances.

'He and his colleague were just here

181

temporarily, though,' her father went on. 'They're off back home now. Pity — I'll miss them.'

* * *

'I hope you don't think it was a wasted journey,' Zara said to Rick as they flew back over the Swiss Alps. 'But it really has set my mind at rest about my father.'

'Good. Perhaps you'll be able to do some work for me now,' Rick said.

'We've lost two days' filming,' she reflected solemnly. 'Harry has been very patient with me.'

'He has. But once he sees those stunt pictures he'll be crowing all the way to the bank and thinking the disruption was all worth it.'

Zara turned and looked at Rick with a puzzled expression on her face.

'Adam made sure all the right papers got the best shots of your little stunt jump and it will set the film up to be the success of the year. And the guy at the top of the steps had the presence of mind to make a spectacular film record of it. Pure magic!'

'Well at least I've done something to please you.'

He glanced down at her. 'Hey! What's with the pathos?'

'It's an occupational hazard, isn't it?' Zara said sadly. 'Leading ladies falling in love with the director?'

Rick's face tightened. 'Yes.'

'And the other way round?'

'Sometimes.' His voice was terse and she couldn't bear to probe further and discover she was just one in a long line of beautiful women he had been attracted to.

'When I've finished this film,' she told him, 'I'm quitting the big time. I'm not cut out for it, the past few days have taught me that.'

'The last few days have shown that you have all the star quality and courage necessary to make a superb career in films,' he said carefully.

'You hate that, though . . . the idea of

the big star on a pedestal . . . '

'Look, when I first met you there were some prejudices I'd been carrying around for far too long, and that was one of them.'

'Will you tell me about it?' she asked softly.

'When I first saw you sailing up the Grand Canal like a queen I was furious with myself for having been lured into the glittering grasp of money and fame. You represented all those things I despised; tasteless publicity, glitzy glamour, and incredible luck.'

Rick lowered his gaze and his voice grew quiet. 'It all goes back to childhood memories . . . ' he began. 'My mother was dumped by my father when I was a kid. He went off with a rich and lucky woman who'd inherited her family's fortune. She'd never done a day's work in her life and she took for granted everything my mother had to struggle for.

'Eventually, he soon stopped sending maintenance money and she was too proud to fight him for it. She went from one dreary job to another to support us, dreadful grinding jobs where exploitation of a woman on her own was rife. She insisted that I had the chance of higher education rather than leave school and get a job as she did. She died just before I graduated, exhausted and so terribly poor.'

Zara held her breath, knowing the story was not finished.

'When I looked at you in that antique gondola, beautiful and young with crowds applauding you, I saw how you were set up for life and I was reminded of the whole damned unfairness of things . . . when you arrived at the reception I was overcome with feelings of resentment. But I was a complete fool and a brute, for even then I saw that you were not only physically lovely, but warm and natural, full of strength and energy. I wanted to get to know you as no one else has ever known you.'

'Who ever loved that loved not on first sight?' she murmured. 'So you really meant it . . . '

'Yes.' He touched her hand lightly. 'But you're not to give up all your chances for me,' he said. 'I'm thirty-six, Zara. I'm at a crossroads in my career. I could be on the road downwards to nowhere — and, yes, I have had my share of brief love affairs that didn't work out, but that's all in the past.'

Happiness surged through her as she grasped the full meaning and sincerity of his words. 'I'd give up anything for you,' she said firmly. 'But there won't be any need, will there? You'll have me as Zara Silk, ordinary or extraordinary — wouldn't you?'

His eyes were dark and serious. 'Yes,' he answered simply.

'I'll finish the film and then I'll do some hard thinking,' she told him.

'About your future career?'

'Of course. I don't have to think about you, Rick. What I feel about you is perfectly simple.' She turned in his arms and drew his head down.

The plane arrived at Marco Polo

airport as the sun was flashing across the Lagoon, Venice beckoning below, but the two passengers were still wrapped in each other's arms. Sometimes even the wonder and fantasy of Venice must take second place . . .

9

Almost a year to the day later, Zara and Rick were in Venice once again for the presentation of *Captive Countess* at the film festival. The Palazzo Del Cinema was brilliant with lights as the star of the film and its director arrived.

Zara was dressed in a simple cream silk gown, with her hair long and loose down her back. As she entered the crowded auditorium Rick placed a gently affectionate arm around her to guide her to her seat.

Harry Salt was already seated, anticipating the film with smiling serenity. He may well appear satisfied; the film had already collected most of the awards on offer on the international circuit and its young star, whom he had discovered and championed, had won herself a glittering reputation.

Benny Proctor lingered in the bar,

celebrating the success that he and his crew had won gaining the award for best photography. Hurrying out of the bar was Adam Leslie, delighted that his client Zara Silk had given a cracking performance in her first big starring role.

Not only that, but she had endeared herself to millions when she went on to marry her director Rick Crane, immediately after filming, in a very traditional fashion in an English country church.

Adam regretted that she had left the international film circuit for a few months, but there was the upcoming season at the National to look forward to next autumn — and with both husband and wife involved. What a publicity coup that would be!

The auditorium fell into an expectant hush as the director and the principal actors moved to take their places before the showing of the film. Within moments the room had darkened and, up on the screen, flashed the words, *Captive Countess*. A Harry Salt film.

Directed by Rick Crane and introducing Zara Silk . . .

And in an anteroom close by, a proud grandfather paced to and fro, cradling in his arms a tiny month-old baby with his father's jet-black hair and his mother's violet eyes.

THE END

We do hope that you have enjoyed reading this large print book.

Did you know that all of our titles are available for purchase?

We publish a wide range of high quality large print books including:
Romances, Mysteries, Classics
General Fiction
Non Fiction and Westerns

Special interest titles available in large print are:
The Little Oxford Dictionary
Music Book, Song Book
Hymn Book, Service Book

Also available from us courtesy of Oxford University Press:
Young Readers' Dictionary
(large print edition)
Young Readers' Thesaurus
(large print edition)

For further information or a free brochure, please contact us at:
Ulverscroft Large Print Books Ltd.,
The Green, Bradgate Road, Anstey,
Leicester, LE7 7FU, England.
Tel: (00 44) **0116 236 4325**
Fax: (00 44) **0116 234 0205**

Other titles in the
Linford Romance Library:

JUST A MEMORY AWAY

Moyra Tarling

In hospital, Alison Montgomery cannot remember her own name. She hears the doctors' hushed whispers — sees their worried glances, which speak of the dark secrets lying just beyond the locked shutters of her memory. Then they bring her the stranger who says he's her husband. But why can't she remember loving a man as compelling as Nicholas Montgomery? And yet the shadows in his eyes clearly reveal that there's something in their past better left forgotten . . .

SECRETS IN THE SAND

Jane Retallick

When Sarah Daniels moves to a sleepy Cornish village her neighbour, local handyman and champion surfer, Ben Trelawny is intrigued. He falls in love with her stunning looks and quirky ways — but who is this woman? Why does she lock herself in her cottage — and why she is so guarded? When Ben finally gets past Sarah's barriers, a national newspaper reporter arrives in the village. Sarah disappears, making a decision that puts her life and future in jeopardy.

WITHOUT A SHADOW OF DOUBT

Teresa Ashby

Margaret Harris's boss, Jack Stanton, disappears in suspicious circumstances. The police want to track him down, but Margaret believes in him and wants to help him prove his innocence. Meanwhile, Bill Colbourne wants to marry her, but, unsure of her feelings, she can't think of the future until she finds Jack. And, when she does meet with him in Spain, she finally has to admit to Bill that she can't marry him — it's Jack Stanton who she loves.